Northwest Vista College
Learning Resource Center
3535 North Ellison Drive
San Antonio, Texas 78251

D1564387

the queen is in the
garbage

Classic Feminist Writers Series

In the Name of Friendship
Marilyn French

A Short Walk
Alice Childress

the queen is in the garbage

LILA KARP

Preface by Lila Karp

Introduction from the 1971 Belmont Edition
by Kate Millett

Afterword by Vivian Gornick

The Feminist Press
at the City University of New York
New York

Published in 2007 by The Feminist Press at the City University of New York
The Graduate Center
365 Fifth Avenue, Suite 5406
New York, NY 10016

Library of Congress Cataloging-in-Publication Data

Karp, Lila.
  The queen is in the garbage / Lila Karp ; with the introduction from the 1971
Belmont edition by Kate Millett and an afterword by Vivian Gornick.
      p. cm. — (Classic feminist writers series)
  Originally published: London: W. H. Allen, [1969].
  ISBN-13: 978-1-55861-538-0 (pbk.); ISBN-10: 1-55861-538-5 (pbk.)
  ISBN-13: 978-1-55861-540-3 (library); ISBN-10: 1-55861-540-7 (library)
  1. Single women—Fiction. 2. Childbirth—Fiction. 3. Mothers and
daughters—Fiction. 4. Man-woman relationships—Fiction. 5. Identity
(Psychology)—Fiction. 6. Feminism—Fiction. 7. Stream of consciousness
fiction. I. Title.
  PS3561.A68Q45 2007
  813'.54—dc22
                              2006100932

This novel was brought to the attention of The Feminist Press at the City
University of New York by Associate Professor Sharon P. Holland in the
Department of African American Studies at Northwestern University.
This publication was made possible, in part, by Northwestern University.

Text and cover design by Lisa Force
Printed in Canada

13 12 11 10 09 08 07   5 4 3 2 1

Dedicated to Renos Mandis
Thanking Claire Russell

PREFACE

As It Was

Conjuring up a sense of myself as a woman who could even dare to envision writing a novel occurred in London around 1965. Before that time, like many women for centuries before me, I had kept voluminous secret journals hidden in bureau drawers. Following a jaunt around Europe, I arrived in London in the early sixties for what I imagined would be a week's visit before returning to New York City. I stayed nine years. Things happened. I got a job writing a monthly column for British *Vogue*. I developed a strong friendship

1

with a British playwright, Jane Arden. She was still swimming in the West End success of her play "The Party." I was floating in the pleasures and panics of an American living a London life during a period of profound social change in England.

It was the Roaring Sixties. The Beatles were roaring. Lucy in the Sky with Diamonds was flying high. Psychedelic Happenings were happening. London fashion was shifting from dowdy to more-than-French-chic. The Labour Party returned to power. New universities opened, giving more and more students state support. The death penalty was abolished. Homosexuality between men over 21 and abortion were both legalized. For the first time the voice of the working class was spewed out to theater audiences in Frank Norman's play "Fings Ain't What They Used To Be." Radical psychoanalysts R.D. Laing and David Cooper were spreading the ideas expressed in their works *The Divided Self* and *The Death of the Family*. Harold Pinter's voice was talking to theater audiences in-between-the-lines in a minimalist voice, and Jean Paul Sartre's play "No Exit" could be viewed on BBC television. Existentialism was not yet a dirty word among intellectuals but rather a much-discussed humanist philosophy. Some contemporary women writers were courageously exploring the struggles, conflicts, and experiences of women in a patriarchal culture. The seeds were being sown for the enormous revival-to-come of the works of earlier women authors such as Jean Rhys and Zora Neal Hurston, to mention just two of my favorite writers. Doris Lessing published *The Golden Notebook*. Sylvia Plath published *The Bell Jar* and then killed herself. Nell Dunne wrote "Poor Cow." Juliette Mitchell was pondering the concepts for her 1971 work "Woman's Estate," and for her important 1974 publication of "Psychoanalysis and Feminism." Jane Arden—my friend had taken on the surname of Shakespeare's mother—could be overheard with me in restaurants, pubs, and tea shops engaging in lengthy conversations about what my future friend, the American academic, Lynn Chancer, in her 1992 book *Sadomasochism in Everyday Life* would label "Engendering Sadomasochism." Jane and I roared about psychic sadomasochism, power and powerlessness between the sexes, women's second-class citizenship in the contemporary world around us, and most importantly, how these factors infiltrated and seeped like poison into our personal lives.

In short, we were exploring ideas that on the other side of the Atlantic were becoming two of the basic concepts of the second wave of the American feminist movement—consciousness-raising and the personal is political. We were not familiar with Betty Friedan's notion of "the problem with no name" as expressed in her 1963 book *The Feminine Mystique*. Instead we were nourished by Simone de Beauvoir's philosophical existentialist look at how, "One is not born, but rather becomes, a woman," proclaimed in her 1949 work *The Second Sex*. That idea, translated into existentialist language, simply means "Existence precedes essence." There is

3

no preordained human nature and therefore certainly no "eternal feminine." Nor, I might add, any "eternal masculine." It was through de Beauvoir's existentialist lens that Jane and I viewed the world around us, and examined how we, as members of the female sex, were personally struggling to overcome the obstacles placed in our path. The battle was clearly between the contradictions of society's messages about women and their place in the world versus our own—often hidden—wishes, desires, and longings.

The "spirit of the age" as Virginia Woolf called it; my personal psychoanalysis with a generous and brilliant woman, Claire Russell; the impassioned taking-off-of-psychic-veils conversations with Jane; and the good fortune and luck of meeting Renos Mandis, a man who encouraged and supported my dreams, all affected my decision to translate some of my life's experiences and struggles towards freedom into art. In 1966 I began to write. The working title for *The Queen Is in the Garbage* was "Confinement."

To jump ahead for a moment. When I came back to live in the United States in 1969 my novel had come out in England and would soon appear in the United States. The idea that the "personal is political" was no surprise to me. It took me only a very short time after my arrival in New York City to become passionately engaged with what I quickly learned was a budding, and in some circles thriving, feminist movement. I had not used the "F" word before that. Here was my opportunity, other than through dialogue and art, to take action and join with others who dreamed of, and were committed to, changing the world. I, along with my new American friends—Kate Millet, Flo Kennedy, Ti-Grace Atkinson, Margo Jefferson, Anne Koedt, to mention just a few—decided, as women, to borrow from Jean Paul Sartre, in his essay "Existentialism Is a Humanism," to choose for every woman that which we chose for ourselves: as much freedom to author our lives as possible. To accomplish this an end to sexism was mandatory.

Finding the Form to Fit the Content

In a discussion of literature Thomas Mann noted that literary works were created from the union of suffering with the instinct for form. While living in London I suffered the death of a premature baby. I don't know about the *instinct* for form but I did want to give shape to, dramatize, and illuminate this experience both for myself and for others. Employing a crisis situation that takes place in the compact time of around 24 hours as the means for revealing the behavior, heart, and soul of a person's past, present, and vision for the future was not new. I joined the good company of the ancient Greek dramatists when I chose to expose the life experiences, conflicts, and psyche of my heroine in the context of her ordeal, giving birth under extremely stressful circumstances. Choosing this crisis situation offered me the opportunity to explore, through a stream of consciousness, how a woman's past—both familiar and historical—affected

5

her present choices and influenced the meaning she would project onto her future.

I am deeply grateful to Professor Sharon Holland for her dedicated efforts to see to it that *The Queen Is in the Garbage* is republished and for enabling this novel to be re-awakened in the twenty-first century. She often used my novel in classes she taught at the University of Illinois in Chicago. The many positive and enthusiastic responses from young students affirmed Dr. Holland's own belief in the historical and personal need to have this novel once again in print. Acting on these feelings she brought the novel to the attention of The Feminist Press, conveying to them its contemporary value. I thank Florence Howe and the editors of The Feminist Press for choosing to consider a republication of *The Queen Is in the Garbage* for their Feminist Classics Series. Hopefully it will bring to the consciousness of new generations the subjectivity of a woman who grew up in the thirties, forties, and fifties, and whose dramatic crisis took place in the sixties. Thanks to many factors, not the least of which was/is my active participation in the second wave of American feminism, I no longer feel confined to the garbage. Nor do I sit in the parlor eating bread and honey. I am not the Virgin or the Whore. Just a woman trying to be a vital human being.

Lila Karp

Santa Monica, California

December 2006

INTRODUCTION FROM THE 1971 BELMONT EDITION

Lila Karp has managed to get it all on paper. For a whole generation of women she has summed up the affairs we've had, the pregnancies and fears of pregnancy, the abortions, the smash-ups—what we've learned while sealed up in the cupboard of our biological definition, as Karp's Harriet is pinned to a table during the long hours of labor. The way we hate and then repeat our mothers' defeated lives: our guilty complicity with our guilty fathers. This novel knows the forces that have conspired to make our lives nervous, anxious, impossible within our precarious seeming-freedom of education, leaving home, travel, taking jobs and lovers. Harriet's childhood is a crisis of guilt and fear and self-loathing, the cumulative triumph of parental attitudes in Apartment 6L, Forest Hills.

This is a new kind of book for a woman to write. Real, therefore unfeminine. There is no reticence here, none of the euphemism we usually retire behind. There will be more books like this, since once we start telling the truth it is difficult to stop. Karp's tight hard little sentences and the ingenuity of a narrative technique which hits upon a period of intense physical pain to free itself of time so that all moments are present in one moment, every memory simultaneously accessible, has reached for and grasped the actuality of a woman's experience. With so much life revealed before us, retreat would now be impoverishment.

Kate Millett

I lie still on the couch. As I was told to. I listen to
Tracy and Sally moving about rapidly in the next room.
Getting dressed and making phone calls.

At last something has happened. I didn't know it
would be at two in the morning. In Tracy's New York
apartment on West 71st Street. But I imagined something would happen. So I lie here scared out of my wits.
Because something is happening. And relieved that it
is. I know that this is only the beginning of a long

night. That will last how long I don't know. But I know that at the end of it something will have happened.

Tracy rushes out of the bedroom. To answer the door bell.

"Come this way. She's in the living room. On the couch."

I look up. See two men standing over me. Smiling.

"We'll carry you down, lady."

"No. No, I can walk. I'm all right. I can walk."

Screaming at the top of my lungs. Kicking with all my eight-year-old might. The man picking me up. After the crash into the tree on my bicycle. 'Put me down. Let me go.' Don't talk to strange men. Ever. They'll harm you. Take advantage of you. Do terrible things to you. Learn to take care of yourself. Women have to. My mother says so.

"Are you sure, lady? There are a lot of steps to go down. It would be much easier for you if the two of us carried you."

"No. I'll walk. To the steps anyway."

Tracy takes my hand underneath the blanket. The motor starts.

Sally says, "I'll show you what to do now. Watch me carefully."

I watch her. Acting as if everything is quite normal. Except that she's in a rush. The school teacher trying to jam twenty minutes of lecturing into the two minutes before the bell.

"Try to forget about everything else," she says. "Now watch. Keep your breathing high. Up here on your chest."

"Yes. I'm sure that's very important," Tracy says. "It is even in Reichian therapy. For relaxation."

I obey.

Mustn't think about what's happening. That won't help. Do what Sally says. Breathe.

"Good," Tracy says. She squeezes my hand.

I listen to the noises of the New York traffic. Familiar sounds.

"What direction are we going in?" I ask. "Uptown or downtown?"

"I think downtown. But I'm not sure," Tracy answers. "Listen, Harriet. As soon as we get there I'm going to call Robert."

"No. Don't do that. Don't call Robert. There's no sense in telling him anything. No sense in worrying him. There's nothing he can do from where he is."

Where is he? Where was he last week? When he let me leave London and come to New York? What am I doing in this city?

"Where are they taking me to, Tracy?"

"I don't know. I didn't ask," she answers. "We'll know soon enough. It can't be too far away."

Something I should be doing. Breathing. Yes. That's right.

I turn my head to the side. See a bit of building stand still as we rush past.

"I know where we are now, Harriet. Downtown. That's the women's prison we're passing," Tracy says. "We're in Greenwich Village."

Don't think about it. Don't think about the weirdness. Of being in Greenwich Village. The women's prison. Passing it every day on the way home from work. Editing children's books. Stopping to shop for dinner on Bleecker Street. For me and Harvey. My husband Harvey. Trying to think and not to think about what life is like for the women inside. Behind bars. And outside. Do they all feel like me behind their burlap curtains on Grove Street? Itchy? Or are some as free as we all look on a sunny day in Washington Square Park? Holding hands with him, just like at the University.

Way before that. Twelve not twenty-one. Escaping to the Village. To breathe the Bohemian air. Get rid of the stifling feeling of Forest Hills, New York. Apartmen 6L is where the hell is. So stay out of it. The world outside is where the fun is. Ben knows that.

In and out of Village book shops with Babs. Pretty Babs with her long black braids. 'Let's tell everyone we're sisters. Even if my hair is dirty blonde.' Looking at the paintings lined up on the sidewalk. Then home.

Back to prison. No later than six. Hoping Jeannie doesn't have one of her fits. About that disgusting, Bohemian, slut-filled Greenwich Village. And keep me from going next Saturday.

'I want you to stop calling me Jeannie. I'm your mother and I want some respect. You hear me, you brat. Respect. Like other children show their mothers. Respect. Your father might think it's cute to be called Ben by the likes of you. Well I don't. I want some respect around here.'

The two of us. Harvey and Harriet. 'Of course we'll live in Greenwich Village, Harriet baby. It's the only place to live in this city.' In our Grove Street apartment. I wonder if he knows I don't really come? Don't tell him you're bugged with the way he treats your friends. Really bugged. As if he can't let anyone else like you. Don't ever scream or get angry like Jeannie. That mouth of hers could scare anybody away. Poor Jeannie. She's got a lot to be angry about. Ben treats her like dirt. Got to make Grove Street better than 6L. All the not telling Harvey. How it's impossible to breathe on Grove Street. Just like it was in the other room. With Harvey in 6L. Always waiting to find out what Harvey feels like doing. Everybody saying how funny it is that I should marry someone with the same name as my brother.

I feel the speed of the engine. Flying me over the

narrow streets of Greenwich Village. And I hear Sally.

"Try and relax, Harriet. Everything's going to be all right. Tracy and I are with you. And you know we love you."

Harvey saying: 'We'll be able to love each other more if we move to the country.' Reds and golds of the country trees in autumn. My beautiful skirt with the same colors in it. Now it will work. In this old spacious house with the early American antiques we keep digging up around here in upstate New York. Harvey was right. It's better if I don't work. If I stay home and cook stews and grow herbs to put into them and sew curtains and nights by the fire and Harvey telling me about the country kids he's teaching and Jock with his floppy ears and giant paws. For me to take care of. Now that's the way it should be. Isn't it? Harvey at work. Me at home. Harvey says so. Now this looks different from 6L.

'I don't know, Jeannie, why you're such a lousy cook.' Ben going on and on about what a great cook his mother is until Jeannie starts screaming: 'What's the good of cooking a meal for a bum who comes home at any damn time and doesn't give a damn about me. You only care about your lousy card-playing friends and loose women. Oh, I know, all right. Why you've been coming in at four every night this week. Out with one of your whores. Lipstick marks all over your goddamn handkerchiefs. That I wash and iron. Don't you think I know? Wining and dining them on the outside. Spending plenty of money on your women and cronies and I have to beg for enough money to run this house. For a couple of dollars to buy some clothes. You're a big-time Charlie on the outside and then you come home at any damn time you please and expect me to wait on you hand and foot. Where are you going? When will you be back?'

Ben sprinkling his handkerchief with cologne. Tucking the fresh white cloth into his pocket. 'I'm going out. I've listened to you enough for one night. You get on my nerves. Can't you ever do anything but shout and holler? I don't know when I'll be back. I just don't know.'

"Do you know where we are now, Tracy?" I ask. "Tell me. Where we are."

"We must be in the lower part of the Village. Don't worry. Maybe we're going to stop right here in the Village."

None of those sounds here. Not for Harvey and me. Here in Skaneateles. Far away from Ben and Jeannie and New York City. Holding hands and walking around the lake. But what am I doing here? With this Harvey who keeps telling me where I'll be able to love better. What the house should look like to love better in. Who we should be with on what night where. Something's wrong and I don't know what it is. But I don't want to to have the baby that goes with the house. Or do I? And it's Harvey who doesn't want a baby now? And I can't stand another minute of this lie and this not being able to say what I want to do. Because I don't know, but I do know that I don't want to be in this house with Harvey. That I've got to get out of here before I die because it feels just like it felt in that room with my brother. Like I've got to hide myself in order to go on living. Protection and the title of Mrs. aren't worth that. I've got to get out.

But I'll be alone again. Remember when my brother went into the Navy. It was worse than when he was in the room. Bossing me around. It will be worse being single. So what? I'm only twenty-four now. I'm pretty. I'm not dependent on Harvey. I've got my own money. Even if I can hardly remember the little man who left it to me. The one I called grandpa and used to watch squirting the juice of his grapefruit all around the table. I can take care of myself. Besides. Harvey will begin to hate me anyway. If I don't do what he wants me to. If I find out what I want and tell him, he'll leave me. So leave him. Before that happens. Go away.

Back again to Greenwich Village. After the divorce. Free. Now they're taking me to a hospital in the Village. As if I never left New York and all that was familiar. Whatever's going to happen is going to happen in New York. Maybe Greenwich Village. What's going to happen? Why am I here? Alone? Where's Robert?

"How do you feel?" Sally asks.

I smile for Sally. "All right. I feel all right."

We swerve around a sharp corner. The siren sounds louder.

"Are we still in the Village, Tracy," I ask.

"No. It looks like we've left it. Like we're going downtown. And towards the East Side."

Leaving the Village. And one night lovers and cafés and drinks with publishing executives telling me how soon I'll be a top editor and have another drink and come back to my apartment for a coffee. I ache. Might as well see something new. Lots of people travel.

Running to Europe. Five years ago. Boats—planes—trains—trucks. Keep moving. Quick fucks. Not enough time together with any man to be afraid of being left alone. Again. Or stuck with someone breathing down my throat so I don't have a chance to know whose saliva I'm swallowing.

Then London. That's where Robert is. In his country. He's in our flat in London. Or out. With who at this minute? Never mind. Don't think about it. Whatever's going to happen is going to happen here. In my home town. It's unexpected and I've been taken by surprise. No worse than all the surprises with Robert these last few months. All the unexplainable surprises. There will be an explanation for this. Don't panic.

"Come on," Sally says. "Try it again now. It's important to develop a rhythm and concentration. Go on. Keep practicing. It will make life so much easier for you later. I promise you."

Harvey saying: 'I've called my cousin's doctor, Harriet. He says to get you to a hospital. That your pains might mean that you're going to have a miscarriage. That you shouldn't move until the ambulance gets here. It will be here very soon. Here are some warm clothes. Put them on and lie quietly. Is the pain very bad?' 'No. It's all right. But I'm bleeding. Badly.'

In the emergency room: 'This will calm you down, Mrs. Stein.' The needle goes in. Blur begins. Being wheeled through the halls. Remembering Jeannie telling me how I was born in this hospital. Saint Mary's.

'They don't like Jews there.'

'Then why was I born there mommy?'

'Because it was the hospital that my doctor worked in. I lost a baby because of him. Off at the race track or drinking or playing cards with his cronies or something like that. I lost four babies before I finally had you. Miscarriages.' And in angrier moments, Jeannie's face distorted with hate: 'If I had known what I was going to get with you I wouldn't have tried to have another baby. I lost four before I finally had you. You brat. Look what I got.'

Being wheeled through those halls. 'Your pains might mean that you're going to have a miscarriage.' Hearing Jeannie's voice screaming at Harvey: 'How do you know that the doctor who's going to operate is any good? I should be making the decision about who's going to operate. She's my daughter. This wouldn't have happened if it weren't for you.' Harvey's rage: 'Listen, Mrs. Battenberg. There's no time now. They're taking her into the operating room. There's no time.' Hearing my brother's voice: 'For God's sake, mother. Be quiet. Harriet's in danger and you're screaming about whose fault it is. Be quiet.'

Lying on that moving slab. More scared of what the doctors and nurses are thinking about my mother's sound than I am of the operation. They'll throw me out of here if she goes on like that. Screaming in hospital halls. They'll throw us all out. They won't take care of me.

The mask. 'That's it, Mrs. Stein. Breathe deeply.' This same hospital when I was six. Being anaesthetized. For an ear operation. 'Where are you taking me?' 'To see the puppies. The cute little puppies.' But there were no puppies in there. Instead they put a muzzle on me. They lied. They said they were taking me to see the puppies. Well I know that mask this time. It's not a muzzle and there's no shock. I don't expect puppies this time. That muzzle contains ether and I'm miscarrying.

Flat bellied. My father sitting beside me. Asking how I feel.

'You look O.K. Really O.K.'

'Yes, Ben. I'm O.K. Where's Jeannie?'

'She's not feeling well. Can't come to see you because she's not feeling well herself.'

'What's wrong with her, Ben?'

'Oh you know. She's got a cold or something.'

Harvey sitting next to me. Holding my hand. How tired he looks.

'I've brought you some magazines. How do you feel?'

'O.K. I'm O.K. Did you stay at my parents' house last night?'

'No I didn't. Your mother said she didn't want me staying there. She did more than imply that it's my fault you had this miscarriage. That I shouldn't have driven you all the way from the country in the M.G. That I'm a baby killer and a daughter killer. I'm telling you, Harriet. That's it. I've had enough of her and if you haven't after the way she's treated you through this then I give up. But I'm not seeing her again. Never. She hasn't even been here to see you.'

'Harvey. Please don't. She's sick, Harvey.'

'She's sick all right. In the head. That's where she's

sick. She's glad this happened. That's what she is. She doesn't want you to have anything. Not me. Not your baby. Can't you see that?'

Leaving New York. Back to the country. Weak. With Dr. Farrow's words jumbling about: 'Sometimes, Mrs. Stein, sometimes nature knows best. Washes babies out that are malformed. Nature does it early. In the third month. Like with you. You're probably very fortunate to have lost that baby now. It was probably malformed. Nature knows best.'

Wondering who nature is and how to account for the thousands of malformed people. And Jeannie's behavior. How to account for that? So it doesn't hurt so much. She's had a lousy life with Ben. That's it. She used to be so beautiful and intelligent. Graduated high school with top honors. I know. She's showed me the certificates. A thousand times. And the photographs. Of the young and beautiful girl Ben married. Ben's made her hateful. Treating her like a piece of furniture. That you bring out after the party in someone else's place. To sit on when you're tired. But it hurts. Isn't there anything right I can do? To make her love me. To let her know that I know that she hurts. So she'd stop. Stop hating me. And Harvey. And the baby that's dead.

'Harriet, can't you understand? That she's glad this happened. That's what she is.'

"Come on, Harriet," Sally says. "You've had a rest. Better to practice the exercises again. They'll be more helpful than any thinking. Try them again. Come on. I'll do it with you. It's keeping up the rhythm that's most important. Now. High up from the chest. Later you can change the rhythm. You'll see what I mean. For now practice it to In-two-three-four. Out-two-three-four. That's it. Concentrate on short, panting type breaths."

"By the time we get to the hospital," Tracy says, "you'll be an expert. You're doing great. For a dress rehearsal."

In Ben's car. Fourteen. On the way to the doctor. Jeannie hissing out: 'You're poison. Always have been and always will be. Everything you touch turns to poison. Those disgusting boils. You've got them because you've got a rotten mind and rotten blood. That's what you've got. Rotten blood. You're contaminated. To think that a daughter of mine would get herself involved with a Negro. How disgusting can you get? To allow a Nigger to kiss you and touch you and God knows what else. What would it be like to have a black baby in this family?'

'There was nothing else, Jeannie. Nothing else. Martin was my friend. You don't have babies from being friends with someone. There was nothing else.'

'If I hear of you seeing him again I'll kill you. Hear? I'll really kill you.'

Ben saying: 'All right now. Leave her alone. She understands by now what she's done.' Oh God. What have I done. It's too late, Ben. Too late. You've already joined her. First time in your life. You hit me. The other night. What for? What did I do. From her I can understand it. But you, Ben. You beat me? Why? Beat me and said I was crazy for doing what I did with Martin. You hit me. For the first time. But what did I do? Kiss Martin? You don't have babies from kissing. Do you?

The boils. Coming all the time after that. Fifteen, sixteen, seventeen. Every year. One after another. Proof of poison blood.

At the doctors. 'Well, Mrs. Battenberg. This treatment should finally cure them. We'll break one today. And reinject some of the serum into her. Principle of a smallpox injection. It's helped lots of teenagers who suffer from boils.'

'You're poison. That's what you are.'

Only a year after the miscarriage: 'I'm afraid, Mr. Stein, that your wife has blood poisoning.'

'Now, Harriet. We're just going to attach these tubes to you. So that you can be fed intravenously. You're a lucky lady. Lucky to be alive. You see. You have a very bad case of blood poisoning. When your husband brought you to the hospital last night you had a fever of one hundred and six. But you're over the worst now. Tell me. Why did you wait so long to get to the hospital? And now that you've lost your baby I think it would be best. I mean, if you told me how it happened. Miscarriages in the second month aren't usually accompanied by such drastic side effects. You don't have to answer me now. I know you're tired. But you think about it. It would help us to know. How you got such a severe case of blood poisoning.'

Talking with Harvey later: 'Did he ask you to tell him what happened, Harvey?'

'Yes. Yes he did. But I think we should just stick to the story. That you started to bleed naturally and began to miscarry.'

'Yes, I agree. No sense in telling them. Maybe we'd get into trouble. If not with the authorities then with those hoods who told us about that midwife. No. Let's not say anything. They'll take the best care of me they can. Won't they?'

'Yes. Of course they will.'

'I don't understand, Harvey. All those people who have abortions with that midwife. But me. I end up with blood poisoning.'

'Don't worry about it now. Just get better. You're off the danger list. Just get strong quickly so you can get out of here.'

Looking at the blood clots in the bed pan. They're poison. Poison blood clots.

Later. Harvey telling me: 'It was horrifying. They thought you were going to die that night. Told me to call your parents. Just in case. Of course I didn't. Your mother would have said that I'd poisoned you or something as evil. God I was scared.'

And wondering. Why didn't he get me to a hospital sooner? Was it because I didn't let on how sick I felt? But it must have been clear. One hundred and six fever by the time he called the ambulance. Thumping the thought to death: He was afraid he'd get thrown out of school if anyone found out I'd had an abortion. More worried about himself than whether I lived or died. And I was afraid. Afraid to frighten him. So frightened that I didn't let on how sick I felt.

The ambulance slows down. I ask, "Are we there yet?"

"No. But we're slowing down," Tracy answers. "I still don't know what hospital we're going to. But we must almost be there."

"Now don't forget," Sally says. "No matter what happens. What they're doing to you. Whether you're answering questions or being examined or what. If you get the contractions, stop everything. And concentrate on the breathing. Forget about the rest of the world and what they're doing. And concentrate on yourself.

And what you must do to help yourself. This is your show Harriet, and don't let anyone confuse you about it."

"Let's hope," Tracy says, "that the doctors and nurses in this hospital are familiar with natural child-birth exercises. That will help a great deal. Now why don't you try them again. In-two-three-four. Out-two-three-four. Keep the panting high and don't forget what Sally said. When the pain starts you just ride it like a wave. Rhythmically. You've already seen what she means. Haven't you?"

"Yes. I have. Like this. In-two-three-four. Out-two-three-four."

"That's it," Sally says. "You're doing great. With that head of yours you'll be doing it in no time. As if you had gone to classes for three months in London. Like you were going to."

That's it. Maybe I'm going to have a baby. Me. Instead of having it in London I'm going to have it in New York. In a hospital whose list I'm not on. With a doctor I've never met. So what? It's as simple as that. I'm about to have a baby. And the ambulance is taking another pregnant woman to a hospital. To have her baby. Prematurely. That woman is me. Lots of women have premature babies. Tracy says I'm going to have a baby. Sally is showing me what to do to make having a baby easier. So I must be going to have a baby. No need to panic. In-two-three-four. Out-two-three-four. That's it. That's the way to have a baby.

Stillness. The sound of sirens stops. This journey is over. Now what?

"All right, lady. You're going to be all right now, lady. We're just going to carry you into the hospital. We're here, lady."

Watching the back of the neck of the stretcher bearer. Carrying a body. My body. Where? Never mind. The pains are starting. Pant-two-three-four. Like a puppy. Out-two-three-four. In-to-this-hospital. Where I'm going to have my baby. I have not had an abortion. I am not miscarrying. The doctor told Tracy on the telephone. That I'm going to have my baby prematurely. That's what Tracy said he said. It isn't as it should have been. London with Robert there. Loving me. But I'm going to have a baby. With-out-two-three-four Robert.

April 14. Soaking up the sun. On the beach in Albufeira. Near the big rock that coiled around the sand like a snake.

"I hate to leave tomorrow," he said. "But the show must go on. How much longer do you think you'll stay here?"

"I'm not sure," she answered. "The rest of this month anyway, and maybe through May. I'd like to finish writing one more short story. And I could use some more of the sun and sea. I'll see how it goes."

"I hope it goes that you come back in May. I know I'll be longing for you."

"I think I'll miss you too."

"When you do get back to London let's start looking for a flat. We've been making it for two years and talking about living together for one of them. So I think it's time we really do it. Let's live together."

"Sure it's not just all this sun and sea, darling?"

"Mmm. I'm sure. I never thought it could be so easy to love someone. I'm sure that I love you and sure that I won't panic out and mess things up like the last time I lived with someone. I never get that killing feeling with you that I used to get with Anna. You know what I mean. The one that goes—Help! I've got to get out of this. I never feel trapped with you. So let's do it. I'm ready to have a permanent address and I want it to be with you."

"And what about my own insanities? I mean when it comes to really living with someone. Home life could still scare the wits out of me. Make me feel like I have to give up my own life. Play dead. For a protection I don't need anyway."

"Come on, darling. You're the sanest person I know. And you know it. And you know how much I want you to work. To write. If for no other reason than that

I'm selfish. I couldn't stand being around a weak woman whose life depended on me. I know we can make it work. In any event come back to London quickly. And don't say I'll see."

"O.K. I'll see. Shall we have a swim?"

"Yes. And then let's go back to the house. I want to start making love to you this afternoon, and not stop until I have to get dressed to catch the plane tomorrow morning."

"That sounds all good. Promise?"

"Promise."

"Come on then," she said. "Enjoy your last swim in sunny-fascistic Portugal."

Dreaming: The man is kissing her on the cheek. 'I'll meet you, my darling girl, at three o'clock in Room 107.' He departs. She walks down the long corridor of doors, searching for the room. 106, 108, 105, 109 appear in their proper order. There is no Room 107. He wouldn't do this to me. He couldn't do this to me. It must be that I misunderstood him. It must be my fault that he's not here.

May 10. Driving through Portugal. Towards Lisbon and planes to London. Away from the Algarve Coast.

Ian concentrated on the winding road. And on cracking peanut shells with his teeth.

Harriet looked through the window at the fleeing fields of mustard. I'm on my way to London, she thought. I've decided to return to London. When I'm by myself I know my decisions are my own. I didn't make the choice for Robert. Or because of Robert. Or to hurt Robert or to please Robert. I was in Albufeira alone and I missed Robert and I've decided to return to London. Not to stay here for another month. It's a great feeling. Knowing that I need Robert. That I want to be with him. Makes me not despise Robert for needing me. Helps me to love him. If I allow this feeling often enough maybe we can cut out a lot of the shit. Maybe I can give up my biscuit game and start to really trust Robert. Maybe I could stop my stone silences with him. When I sit on my throne and watch him trying to figure out what would please me most. A new pair of slacks, a lamb chop with lots of fat on it, a glass of pernod, a discussion about something I've read. I try to make Robert work out what he can do to please me just to make sure he's concentrated on me. And I end up despising him for needing me in that way. If he tries to please me hard enough and often enough I reward him with pleasing him. Being nice. Giving him a biscuit. All to reassure myself that he's focused on me. Anything to make sure that I exist for him at every minute. As if I'd disappear if I didn't. What a bore. When I'm not playing that game I genuinely love him. And want him as a partner and don't despise him for needing me. I'm not doing too badly. For this century, that is. Thirty-one and on my way to knowing and trusting myself. And Robert.

Ian said, "I'm getting a bit tired of driving. Want to stop at a café in the next town for a drink?"

"Yes. Let's do that," Harriet answered. "And give me the bag of nuts. I'll make life easier for you and crack some open. What a way to stop smoking."

"Thanks."

Eating and drinking brandies in the café. Fifty miles outside of Lisbon.

Harriet ran her finger around the rim of her brandy glass. Sleeping together is in both of our heads, she thought. If he pressures me I won't do it. I don't have to do anything I don't want to. I don't have to sleep with him just because he expects me to. But I can do what I want to do. To please myself. To act in any other way, would be as Jean-Paul says, in bad faith.

Ian caught her eye. "I would much rather stay here with you tonight than continue driving up to Lisbon. But I haven't had too much I can't drive. What would you like to do?"

"Stay here with you."

"Good. Let's have another brandy."

Dreaming: Of sitting on a beach with a young man. 'There will be a room for us,' he says, 'and a room for the twins, and a playroom for all of us.' Harriet gets enraged. What the hell makes him so certain that I'll have twins? 'You Americans,' she says, 'you always want a family playroom. The idea disgusts me. I want a room for myself where I can be alone and work. I don't want your family playrooms.'

May 11. Arriving in Lisbon. Peopled pavement and honking horns replaced stretches of green and country silences.

"If it's all right with you," Ian said, "I'll just pop into my newspaper office for a minute and let them know I've got the story of Lennon on the Algarve all ready to send out to London. Then we can have a long lunch and I'll drive you to the airport."

"That's fine with me," Harriet said. "I'll wait for you in the car while you go to your office. I don't feel like confronting the sex starved Lisbon men by myself at the moment. I always end up feeling humiliated. Which I guess is their intention. More or less."

"O.K. I won't be long."

Harriet turned her attention to the finger nails she'd let grow under the sun. I will not bite them in London like I always do. I've said that before. Well in any case I'll try not to. About last night. I made a choice. No one forced me to do anything I didn't want to do. I chose to sleep with a relative stranger. And now I know how meaningless it was. I received and gained nothing from that experience. Besides. He came too quickly. Stop it. Don't send up your own thoughts. The fact is that we created a night not to be referred to. That's choice for you. I wonder if Robert's made it with anybody. If he has I hope he's come out the same side as I have. At least I know I didn't make it with Ian against Robert. Or to prove my independence.

Ian jumped into the car. "O.K.," he said. "They know I'm alive and they've got the scoop on Lennon. Enough work for one day. Let's eat. I'll take you to a tipico Portuguese restaurant. Is good?"

"Very good. I'm hungry."

The two stretcher bearers arrange my body on a long narrow table. One of them says, "There you are, lady. You'll be comfortable now. The doctor will be here soon."

I ask, "Where are my friends?"

"They're at the Bursar's Office. They'll be here just as soon as they're finished admitting you."

The stretcher bearers disappear. A nurse appears. She closes the door of the tiny room. She smiles. Hands me a white hospital smock and politely tells me to put it on.

"How long have you been pregnant?" she asks.

"About seven months."

"Don't worry. Hundreds of premature babies are born that early. The doctor will be here in a minute to see you. Let me help you undress."

"Hello. I'm Doctor Parker. And this is my intern, Doctor Sachs. Tell me, how do you feel?"

"Scared."

"There's nothing to be frightened about. Lie down please and let's have a look at you."

His hands travel over my belly. Gently and in search of information.

"Your friends tell me that you live in London. That you're just back here in New York visiting for a few weeks."

"Yes. Yes, that's right."

Cold steel instrument on my belly. Discovering what?

"And your husband? He's in London now, is he?"

"No. I mean yes, he's in London. But he's not my husband. I'm not married."

'Listen, kid,' coming through my father's cigar. 'I don't know why you always have to tell the truth. Why the hell don't you be like me? Do what you want on the outside. Go to the movies with whoever you want to. But come home and keep your big mouth shut. That's your trouble. You've got a big mouth. You don't know how to keep anything to yourself or how to tell a few white lies. Your mother doesn't have to know the truth. With her kind it only makes trouble. Be like me. Lead your own life. Do what you want on the outside but keep your big mouth shut.'

Cigarless Doctor Parker says, "I see. Well, it's too bad that he's not here with you."

I become the poor, helpless, unprotected, unmarried mother I imagine Doctor Parker sees.

'Men will use you and then toss you away like a dirty old rag. It's the woman who ends up suffering. Who gets pregnant and left with a baby to bring up by herself. Men are after one thing and one thing only and don't you ever forget it.'

'Listen, kid. Don't you think it's time you settled down? You've sown your wild oats, and that's good. I did the same when I was a boy. But there comes a time when you've got to settle down. So you made a mistake the first time. Get married again. Get someone to take care of you. Look after you. Have a few kids. Like I did. It's high time you got married.'

A stethoscope on my chest. And Doctor Parker's voice again.

"Do you have any relations here in New York?"

"Yes. My parents live here."

Doctor Parker smiles. "That's good."

Jeannie and Ben coming to see me at Tracy's apartment. Four days ago. Watching their reactions. Jeannie saying: 'I can't understand. Why if you love someone and are going to have their baby do you come all the way to New York now? By yourself? Just for a few weeks? Why haven't you gotten married? If it's a girl, I want you to name it after my mother. Your brother said he would name his baby after her. But he didn't. Beatrice made sure of that. Went and named it after someone in her family. But don't you forget, Harriet. The woman has first choice. That's one thing the woman does have. First choice. Even in that country you're living in now. So make sure it gets named after my side of the family. My mother, who I loved so dearly, if it's a girl. Isn't your skirt too short? For a pregnant woman?'

Ben saying: 'You're still a wierdy, aren't you, kid? Still got to be different. If you think you're going to get married, and believe you me you ought to, why didn't you just lie? You should have told your mother that you're already married. She's gone all crazy now. And I'll have to listen to her rave about it. All day and night. She'll never stop.'

If not my mother's voice then my father's. Seesawing between not thinking like either one of them. The dizziness of it all.

Doctor Parker hands the stethoscope to Doctor Sachs. "Well, Harriet. You've got a good sized baby in there. At least it certainly seems that way from my examination. And it looks like you're on your way to having it now."

I feel relief. The same feeling I shoved aside when the blood stains first appeared. Something is about to happen. Something unexpected and maybe something dangerous. But something definite and real. Better than all those months of nightmare days.

"What happened, Doctor Parker?" I ask. "Why am I here? What started all this?"

"The placenta has separated from the wall of your womb and labor has begun. There's nothing we can do to stop it now because the contractions have started."

"Does it always work that way? For other women, I mean?"

"No. It doesn't. Sometimes when a placenta begins to separate we can put the mother to bed. But in your case labor has begun. So you're on your way. I don't think there's anything to worry about. Like I said. I have the feeling that your baby is quite well developed for its young age. Now you just try and relax, Harriet. It's nearly three in the morning and it doesn't look like you had much sleep before you got here. Doctor Sachs is going to ask you some questions for our records. Then the nurse will help to prepare you. I'll be close by if you need me."

"My friends. The ones who came here with me. Where are they?"

"They'll be here in a few minutes. By the way. They told me that you know the breathing exercises for easing the pain. And they've asked if our staff knows the natural childbirth procedure. Well, they do. So the nurses will be helpful. And Doctor Sachs also. I'll leave you with him now."

I watch Doctor Parker gently close the door.

Ben slamming the door in Jeannie's face. Storming out of the house after one of their battles. 'I don't know, Jeannie, and I don't care when I'll be back.'

I rush into our room. Harvey's and mine. But it's really Harvey's room. Hoping Harvey is there. Even if he's reading. Just to know he's there. To protect me. She doesn't yell at Harvey. I wonder why? Poor Harvey though. He's so thin and fragile. Always sick. Needs me to be nice to him. Ben isn't nice to him. He ignores Harvey.

'Get out of here, Harriet. I want to read. By myself. I don't want you in here making noise. Why don't you shine my shoes?'

'O.K. O.K. Harvey. I will. Anything else you want me to do for you? Let me stay in here. I'll be quiet. Really quiet.'

'O.K. But don't you dare put your thumb in your mouth. I can't stand the sound of you sucking your thumb. And make sure to keep still.'

Doctor Sachs takes a pen out of his starched white pocket. The nurse hands him the school-entrance job-application rent-a-flat form for filling out.

This time it's a hospital-entrance form. They're going to classify me now. If I die they'll know who died.

My daddy doesn't know me. He doesn't know his own daughter. Sitting up in my crib. In the hospital ward with ten other little girls. Watching Ben enter the room. Dying for a long minute. Turning to stone as I watch him not notice me. He's headed towards some other child. He doesn't know me. He knows his little girl has had her tonsils out but he doesn't know who his little girl is. My daddy turning around, after smiling at the child in the crib next to mine. Saying: 'Hey kid. Look what I've brought you. Lots of crayons and coloring books.'

"I'd like you to answer some questions," Doctor Sachs says. "Just routine questions for our records. Address while here in New York?"

"90-23 . . ."

Why am I reciting my parents' address? I'm not staying with them. I haven't lived there since I'm seventeen. I'm staying with Tracy. Give her address.

"That's wrong. It should be 248 West 71st Street."

The pain is starting again. Stop everything. Start breathing. It doesn't matter if you don't do what he's asked you to. You don't have to shine his shoes or answer his questions this minute. Concentrate on yourself. He won't get angry. Or forget about you. In-two-three-four and Out-of-long-corridors-of-halls. Playing with the gang of kids in the alleyways between apartments. Into Josephine's apartment. 5L.

'Yes, Mrs. Mazzoni. Thanks, Mrs. Mazzoni. I can stay for lunch.' Wondering where my mother is. Why can't I get into my apartment? Why doesn't my mother cook nice things like Mrs. Mazzoni? Where is my mother? There's nobody home in my house.

'Can I wash the dishes, Mrs. Mazzoni?' What can I do to make you like me? To make you see how glad I am you're feeding me. Tell me. I'll do anything to make you care about me, Mrs. Mazzoni. Or even for you, Sammy's mother. Or for you, Ruthie's mother.

Playing games in the halls. 'I'll be the teacher because I'm older than all of you. Now. Everybody take hands in a circle.' Skipping around and singing:

> *The King was in the counting house*
> *Counting out his money*
> *The Queen was in the parlor*
> *Eating bread and honey*

Tripping on a yellow jelly bean. Holding my head. The blood rushing out of it onto my hand. Ringing the bell. No answer. I better go to Mrs. Mazzoni's. She'll take care of me.

Mrs. Mazzoni holding my hand while the seven stitches are woven into my head.

"Has the pain subsided now?" Doctor Sachs asks.

"Yes. It has."

"You do the breathing exercises quite well. Did you go to classes in London?"

"No. My friend. The one who brought me here. She's had four babies. She showed me how to do it in the ambulance."

"You certainly caught on quickly. You do them very well."

'You're too smart you brat for your own good. Hear?' Jeannie shouting: 'That's what you are. Too smart for your own good.'

'Your brain and a nickel will get you a ride on the subway and that's about all.' Ben laughing: 'Except into a lot of trouble.'

"Your age, Harriet?"

"Thirty-two."

My brother, he's seven years younger than me. I mean older. I always make that mistake. He seems younger. He's so frail. Jeannie says so. Needs to be treated gently. Taken care of as if he was my kid brother. As if I'm his mother and he's my little boy. My little frail boy. Do it with anybody. Brothers-cats-dogs-children. Treat them the way I long to be treated. Protect them. Do anything. But don't think about myself. How it hurts. Where it hurts.

'You're hurting me, Harvey. Stop hitting me. You're hurting me.'

'Well then stay out of my way in here. You're a clumsy kid. You should have seen my model airplane drying on the floor when you walked in here and stepped all over it. It's ruined now.'

Over the years. Learning to survive in that tiny room with Harvey. Play make-believe. Make believe I'm not here. Look at the pretty colored flowers on the rug and remember there's a beautiful world outside this room. Filled with beautiful flowers. And beautiful people. Hide in here. Jump up on the nearest shelf and hide. So he doesn't see or hear me. Watch Harvey's every mood. Know what to expect and what he wants. Keep my eyes on Harvey.

'I've told you before, you brat, to hide your body in front of your brother. Men are men even if he is your brother and if you go about flaunting yourself at him he'll end up doing something to you that he doesn't want to. Don't you dare walk around in your slip in his room anymore. You're eleven years old now. Not a baby anymore. You're a young lady. And your brother is eighteen. Get dressed in the bathroom and don't dare expose yourself to your brother ever again. And remember. Your brother is and always will be the best friend you ever had. He's your own flesh and blood. He's the same as you.'

Harvey getting out of bed in the morning. In his underpants. Don't look at that thing hanging there. He's my best friend but I'm not supposed to see that thing. I wish we had our own rooms so I wouldn't have to look at what it's bad to look at. And so he couldn't see me. And my every move. Why are we living together? Like Ben and Jeannie live together in the next room. Why doesn't Ben tell Jeannie we should have different rooms?

"Any miscarriages?" Doctor Sachs asks.

"Yes. One."

'For God's sake, Harriet. Answer me. I've told you, baby. I'm sorry, baby. I didn't mean to slap you. It's just that you exasperated me today with all that silence of yours. It was stupid of me to lose my temper. Especially as you're pregnant. Tell me you forgive me. It's never happened before and it'll never happen again. It's me. Harvey. Your husband. I'm trying to talk to you. Answer me, Harriet.'

I never should have given up the scholarship for my Masters Degree because of this pregnancy. I don't want a baby with Harvey. Don't answer him. If I do I'll scream like Jeannie. And he'll hate me. Don't do that. Just keep silent.

'Sometimes, Mrs. Stein, sometimes nature knows best. Washes babies out that are malformed.'

"Any abortions?"

"Yes. I had one after the miscarriage."

Harvey doesn't really want me to have a baby. But then why am I married to him? What am I doing with him? I should have a baby. I'm not working now. Not since Harvey suggested that I don't work so that he can feel like the man. I'm going to suggest that I have an abortion. Maybe he'll beg me to have the baby. If he does I will.

"Any complications with either?"

"Yes. Blood poisoning with the abortion."

"I see. The father's name and address?"

"Robert Felton. 80 Stanley Gardens."

"And telephone number?"

"Bayswater 6439."

'Yes. This is Harriet Stein speaking.' Talking to Robert about eight hours ago. 'I'm fine Robert. Just fine. The baby? Well I get the feeling it wants out of me. Yes. Kicking and pressing on my ribs. As if it can't stand another minute in me. Tonight? I'm going to see some friends in the Village. And you? Happy Christmas Eve to you too.'

Christmas Eve. I wonder how these doctors feel about

taking care of me tonight? Sachs must be Jewish. Then it's not so bad. But the nurses and Parker. They're not. They want to be home with their families. Not here taking care of me.

"And your parents or next of kin. Could you give me their name and address?"

I never die for Jeannie. Not on passports or any other documents. It's always Ben I imagine being told of my death. Suffering. If I die, I'll die for Ben.

"Yes. Benjamin Battenberg. 90-23 145th Street. Forest Hills, New York."

"Thank you," Doctor Sachs says. "That's all the information I need."

He's every Jewish mother's dream of what her son should be. I'm in New York City. Home of all the My Son the Doctor jokes. But he's real. He's real and I'm really here.

'If you'd stop running around with all those Bohemians and communist artists you'd be a lot better off. Get a good Jewish professional man. Someone who treats women decently and with respect. Stay away from Bohemians and bums like your father. You see what kind of a husband he is.'

The nurse approaches me with a small steel basin of water with a sponge floating on top.

"I'm just going to shave you now. It doesn't hurt, so don't worry," she says. "Just lie still now."

47

'Want me to do that for you, darling? I'm more of an expert than you.'

'O.K. Robert. But be careful. It's only the hairs I want shaved off. While you're at it, darling, get those six famous hairs on my belly button. The ones you wrote a song about last year.'

'You're so wet inside. I love it when you're all wet like that inside and I just slip into you.'

'And outside, darling. Let's turn the shower water off. And be careful. It's slippery making love up against a tile wall.'

"And we have to get your stomach empty also," the nurse says. "It makes it more comfortable later."

Leaning over my mother's knee. Jeannie sitting on the bathtub ledge. Holding me down. Trapped in her clutches. Helpless. Humiliated as the tube gets shoved up my anus. Thinking that it's better not to get sick. I'll never get sick again. I swear it.

'And to Harriet Battenberg, the award for perfect attendance during the fifth grade term.' Curtsying at the Principal of P.S. 82. Taking the white certificate with the golden ribbon from his hand.

"You're a good patient," the nurse says. "Some women get a bit hysterical during this part. This is the last of it. You can lie back and relax as soon as you're empty."

She helps me to get off my table. Walks me down

the hall to a line-up of toilets neatly hidden by swinging doors.

I sit on the toilet. And I wonder if the excruciating pain I feel is the beginning of a series of contractions or the result of the enema. Never mind. Don't think. Practice. Breathe-two-three-four. Out-two-three-four. Pray that these pains aren't contractions and that they don't start again now. That would be too ridiculous. Life can't be that absurd. I can't get contractions on a toilet seat while I'm shitting my insides out.

'Open that door,' Jeannie shouts. 'You can't stay in there all day.' Sitting on the wooden toilet top covered in green cloth. Thankful that I reached the bathroom. Got the door locked before Jeannie caught me. Slapped me around some more. Waiting. Long enough for her to cool down. Sneak out and hope that I don't get a bashing. Hope that Ben comes home soon. I want my daddy.

Not knowing that my daddy is having his Sunday shave. After his Sunday bath. Finding the bathroom door open. Walking in. Stunned by seeing Ben there. Naked. I see that same thing like Harvey's. Hanging there. Angry-faced Ben with a razor in his hand. Growling: 'What the hell are you doing in here? I'm in here. Go on. Get out. What are you doing in here when you know I'm in here.' Wondering what made Ben scream like that. I thought there was no one in there.

The door wasn't locked. So why did he get so angry? Wanting to tell Ben. That I really didn't know he was in there. Somewhere knowing not to mention anything about it. Ever.

Older and using the floor of the bathroom as the only safe place to masturbate. Keep the water tap running. 'Yes, Harvey. I'll be out in a minute. Just washing my hands.' *And then Rhett Butler threw her down on the bed and ripped her clothes off.*

"Are you all right in there, dear?" The soft sweet voice of the nurse.

"Yes I am," I answer meekly. "But I'm bleeding a little."

"That's normal. Don't worry," the nurse responds.

Just a few hours ago in Tracy's flat. Tracy asking: 'Are you sure they were blood stains on your panties, Harriet? This isn't some kind of a false alarm, is it?' Trying to pretend that I don't know how disappointed Tracy will be. If the pains and blood don't really mean a birth. So that Tracy can take over. Arrange everything. Be there when the man isn't. Supervising and controlling. Proving that women can do it by themselves. She'd like to have the baby for me. To make up for all of her abortions and mine and everyone else we know. She'd like to do it for me. She can't. They're my blood stains. But she's determined to take over. That's second best. God. They're my stains. What's happening to me?

'Yes, Tracy. I'm sure they're blood stains. You better call a doctor. Right away. I'm scared. I don't know what's happening.'

Insides out, I walk weakly back to my room. The nurse helps me up onto my table.

I wonder how old she is? Around twenty-two. What made her decide to be a nurse? Did she want to be a doctor but decide to leave it to the men? And only play the part of doctor's helper. Does she care or is she just filling in time? Until she finds a good doctor to marry? She's pretty. Even with that Florence Nightingale smile of hers.

"There dear," she says. "We'll be letting you rest now. I'm just going down the hall to see how some of the other women are. Looks like there are going to be lots of little Jesuses born this year."

June 7. Slipping through Sussex countryside. Headed towards the Magic Flute and the Gardens of Glyndebourne.

Harriet asked, "Will we get there on time? I wouldn't want a repeat performance of the last time I started out to hear an opera at Glyndebourne. Got there in time for the last act."

"Don't worry, darling. We're in good time," Robert said. "To tell the truth. Know what I feel like doing?"

"No. What do you feel like doing, Robert? A short walk down one of these country lanes?"

"No, my darling. A quick fuck in one of these country lanes."

"Come on, Robert. It might not be a Dior gown I'm wearing, but I'm not going to get my dress all smudged and wrinkled on the grass."

"Who said anything about the grass? We can do it right here in the car."

"There's not enough room, silly. This isn't a Bentley."

"Oh come on, Harriet. I've wanted to make love to you this whole trip."

"You're sure we won't be late?"

Driving down a country lane. Off the main road. Stopping the car.

"If I come in this position, Robert, it will be a miracle. Or that I love you very much."

"And I love you, Harriet. Go on my darling. I want you to come."

"Now Robert. Now. Hold me. Tightly."

July 10. Leaving Doctor Chander's office. Walking down Seymour Street. Searching for a cab.

Harriet thought, Me! I'm pregnant. Chander says it would be dangerous to have another abortion. Why the hell am I thinking about it that way? Maybe I don't want an abortion. Maybe I want to have this baby. Not so loud. Somebody might hear me. And not so fast. Think about your past scenes with babies. Miscarriages, blood poisoning, and hideous abortions. So what? I was a different person then. I didn't know who I was and what I was frightened about. Too busy thinking about what life should be. And I didn't dare question what was wrong with what was. I thought I was a freak for not staying married to Harvey. I was so focused on him and he was so focused on himself how could we have made it? It's different now. Robert knows my fears. From abandonment to annihilation. And he digs me for not submitting to all the past clichés about little women and big men. He loves me. Or is it really different? What about the way he started running around when his son was born. He really did Anna in. And he's been a lousy father to Jimmy. But he's changed a lot since then. Everybody says so. His friends have even stopped calling him The Shadow. And he told me himself about his flipping out with Anna when Jimmy was born. How he got so frightened. Felt trapped and ended up taking it all out on Anna. So he knows what he's been like. And he's changed. I've seen that myself. He's said that if I ever got pregnant he'd want the baby. He's said he's sure he's ready not to destroy a good thing. And I've been liking myself enough to want to make something that looks like me.

54

There are no miracles, of course, and both of us know it. So we're ready to try and make a scene work. We've at least admitted that. Last month I decided to live with Robert. That was my way of really committing myself to him. So why shouldn't I do something I want to do. Have a baby. This is a hellish time for women. And men. But Robert and I have seen a little light. Out of necessity we'll make it work in a new way. We're both stifled by the old ways. I'm not going to let all of my past failures, or histories for that matter, fuck it up this time. Cool it. See first. See Robert's reaction first. Now that there's a real baby in me. See his reactions.

"Taxi!"

Afternoon dreaming: She is holding a beautiful, black doll in her hands. Its appearance, except for its size, is that of a young woman. She stares with awe and comments: 'How exquisite her face is. How perfectly molded her body is.' She notices the diamond on the lower left eye lid. 'She must be a princess. A princess from an African tribe.' The shadowy figure near her speaks: 'That woman came from a civilization that strove for perfection. Just look at the size of the results.' Harriet holds the doll on her lap. It wets her skirt. She hopes it won't begin to shit all over her. She puts it down on the floor. The beautiful figure becomes an ugly little animal. It claws and grasps its way up onto Harriet's lap. She helps it up, but is repulsed by the ugly creature. I must get rid of this animal, she thinks. She sees the woman hovering about her. That woman knows what I'm thinking. She can read my thoughts and understand my language. I'm afraid she knows that I don't want this animal. Again Harriet holds the beautiful doll in her arms. Again she admires it and again the sneering voice says: 'She tried to achieve perfection. Just look where it got her.' The doll quickly changes back into the clawing, monkey-like animal. It clutches Harriet. She holds it. The head and body of the creature begin to transform in her hands. The head shrinks to the size of a nut. The body becomes flat and one dimensional. It dissolves into a liquid-like substance. Harriet is horrified at the sight. Yet, she thinks, this amorphous form in front of me is like a sculpture. It's an artist's idea of a human being, and it's beautiful.

Sitting in the pub. Surrounded by the nine o'clock drinkers.

Harriet gazed at the coal fire and heard Doctor Chander's afternoon words, "Try drinking Guiness or wine when you go out to the pubs now. Guiness especially. It's healthiest for you when you're pregnant."

"Hello, darling," Robert said. "Sorry I'm late. Got held up at rehearsal. What will you drink?"

"A brandy and ginger, thanks."

Robert returned with a smile and the drinks.

"How's the rehearsing going?" Harriet asked.

"Too early to say. But it's certainly a better part than the one I had in that last play. I'm glad you talked me into taking it. You'll make a star out of me yet. Did you write today?"

"No. I went to see Chander."

"What's the matter? You look great to me. Did you feel sick or just go along for one of his sexy vitamin injections?"

Harriet erased all expression from her face.

"Neither. I went to find out the results of the pregnancy test I took a few days ago. My period was very late."

Robert dropped his eyes. He gazed at his glass of wine. "You didn't tell me you were worried or that you were going for a test."

He removed a package of cigarettes slowly from his jacket pocket. Took one out. Played with it. Concentrated on the motions of lighting it.

"Well, what did Chander have to say?" he asked.

He's scared, Harriet thought.

"That I'm preggers," she said.

Robert stared at his cigarette. Flicked ashes onto the

floor. Took a long drag. Finally, he turned his eyes towards her and smiled. "What with you using words like preggers, my darling, this baby isn't going to have a trace of an American accent. Better watch that. I like the way you say 'dawg.' You do want to have it. Don't you?"

"Not if you don't. Not if it frightens you. I could get rid of it you know. You looked so peculiar when I told you."

"I was surprised that's all. It's not like you to have had a test and not have told me. I was a bit shocked, that's all. I know you want to have it. Don't you?"

"I could get rid of it you know. If you're not sure you want it. I don't want to have a kid by myself. It's a long time since I was filled with the idea that if I didn't have a kid I'd die of unfulfillment and freakhood to boot. I don't need a baby anymore. At least not to prove myself. I'd have to have you with me all the way, and I'd have to know that you really want it. I don't want to have a kid alone."

"What are you talking about, silly? You're not alone. You're with me. We're looking for a flat to live in together. Remember? And I want your kid. Our kid." He waited a moment. "Don't you?"

"Yes I do. Very much. But I could have an abortion. I don't want to, but I could have one. You looked so scared when I told you. This is so serious and you start joking around about American accents."

"Like I said, I was a bit shocked. And I know it's serious. Maybe that's what scared me a bit. My automatic reaction to serious is always one of panic. You know that. It took me a minute to remember what you seem to have forgotten also. That I love you and want you, and that I know you don't need a kid to prove yourself, and that we're together and that we've been together for a long time, and that you're silly."

"And frightened," Harriet said.

"Of the past, and this is now. For both of us. I'm with you, darling. Come on. Let's celebrate with some champagne."

"Make mine a Guiness. Chander says so."

"Tomorrow, mum. Champagne now. And tomorrow we'll call the agent. Tell him we need a bigger flat. For the three of us."

Me. I'm going to have a baby, Harriet thought.

Dreaming: She sits on a lawn and watches a fat, ugly woman talking with her young daughter. Listening to their words, she struggles to figure out what the mother wants. What the daughter feels. 'Amuse me,' the mother says. 'Play the games I suggest. Read comic books.' Meekly, the daughter responds, 'I don't want to join in your games. There is, of course, such a thing as freedom.' The mother spits at the girl's face and kisses an elder daughter. Harriet finds herself engaged in a quarrel and fist fight with the mother. Knowing that the woman's size and strength could kill her, she says, 'I can't continue to fight with you today because I have a wounded hand. You couldn't possibly want to fight with someone who is at such a disadvantage.' The woman persists in the struggle. Harriet sees a group of girls sitting together. The young daughter is among them. Harriet knows the girl is frightened. Her mother might find out that she's been writing her thoughts down on paper. The girl puts her feet together under a table and hides her writing. The mother quickly approaches her. The daughter screams in terror: 'My feet, my feet. I've been putting out burning cigarettes with my feet.' The mother reaches the girl. She gets down on her hands and knees and with an expression of ecstasy she crawls about stamping out the tiny fires.

July 31. Examining the new flat.

"Let's make this the nursery," Harriet said. "It's a good size room for a kid. Lots of space to play around in, and there's no one underneath to disturb. Let's have the floors scraped and the walls painted white. So it can draw or shit all over them. Anything it wants to do in its own room."

Robert smiled. "Shades of reversing the Harvey and Harriet story of sharing one room. Isn't it?"

"You bet," Harriet said. "And listen, Robert. It would make a great room for me to write in until it shows its face. Later I could move upstairs into the small room."

"Good idea. And how about we stop calling it It. How do you like Mozart?"

"I vote for Glyndebourne. It's more feminine. I did mention I'm hoping for a girl."

"Yup. You did. Me too."

Dreaming: Of entering a shop with her mother and father. Harriet asks the shopkeeper to give her some cool, refreshing bath salts. He hands her a large, beautiful jar filled with gloriously colored stones. She examines the stones carefully, and realizes that they are diamonds and rubies. Her delight is disturbed by thoughts that perhaps she is angering her mother. Perhaps the salts are expensive, and perhaps she shouldn't ask to have them. Perhaps they're too good for her. The mother starts screaming: 'You've only brought me in here, Ben, to get me a box of chocolates. A box of worthless chocolates.' Harriet rushes to her. Shaking her mother, she says, 'That's not true, that's not true.

Don't hit me, but that's not true.' Harriet wonders: Will Ben protect me if Jeannie attacks?

August 15.   Laughing and loving and talking.

"Maybe it goes with pregnancy," Harriet whispered. "Maybe there's a change inside me that makes love making so great now. I don't know, Robert. But it's never been so good for me before. Not with anyone. Ever. Do more of that darling. Yes. Go high up into me."

"Like that?"

"Mmm. Just like that."

"That's it, baby. You go. I can feel you on your way. Go on."

"I don't want to come yet, Robert. It feels too good. Are you all right? For a while?"

"I'm fine. Take your time, my darling. Because it's never been so good for me either. Go on. Don't stop. There's more for later. So go on. Take your time and come."

Sucking dry the sensation of climbing. Harriet wound her legs around Robert.

"Come with me, Robert. Come with me now."

Smoking cigarettes.

"It's good with you, Robert. Very good. So good it

makes me sad to think about all the women who don't come. And even worse about those who pretend they do. Like I used to. How do you think Glyndebourne likes it?"

"Makes a change. She probably gets pretty bored in there. Just floating about all day. By the way. Did I tell you how great I felt when you told Kathy and Nick about the baby in you? It was sort of like announcing our engagement. Let's get married, darling."

"Easy going, Robert. Moving into a flat together. Being pregnant. All within a few months. Let's not leap into things too quickly. After all. Like you said, we've just announced our engagement."

He laughed. "If you put that cigarette out, and think you can stand it, I think I'm going to make love to you again."

"I think I could stand it. All night."

"Good. Move over here then. I'm going to turn you over and love you into exhaustion."

August 16. Changing dreams.

From: Mothering a baby that thoroughly resembles a baby ape.

To: Mothering a baby who looks like other babies. With hair only on its head.

• • •

August 30. Lunching with Tracy. In Soho. At Mario's
new restaurant.

Harriet looked around the restaurant. Wondering if
friends thought she was putting on weight or if it was
apparent that she was pregnant.

"I hope they know I'm going to have a baby," she
said. "I want everybody to know. Makes it more believ-
able for me."

"I was so gassed to hear about your belly," Tracy
said. "If you can do it then I'll know I can one day.
Maybe even I can get to realize that having a baby
doesn't mean getting all the lousy treatment that women
through the centuries have worn like a glove. Watch
out. I'm on the me-me-me-story. What I want to hear
about is you. Did Robert and you decide to have a kid?"

"Not exactly, Tracy. We didn't sit down in the parlor
one day and while sipping tea out of porcelain cups
decide to make a baby. But I wasn't wearing my dia-
phragm one afternoon and Robert goofed. Didn't get
out of me in time. In answer to your question. Yes. I
guess we did choose. You know I don't believe in acci-
dents."

"Nor do I," Tracy said. "When will you two get
married?"

"I'm thinking about it," Harriet answered. "I'm not

even sure that I want to get married. What I've really got to concentrate on at the moment is myself. Not giving myself up, that is. I've got to be careful now, Tracy. More careful than ever before that I don't start mixing things up. Like having a baby with being an imprisoned, dead, hating chick, who's bound to either submit all the way, or to play that hellish role of turning into a shrewish monster. It's more important that I write through this pregnancy scene than it's ever been before. I'm going to try and finish that book of short stories I started last year. I've got seven months before the baby is born."

"Your baby will be born without you doing anything. I envy you, Harriet. But what about a simple answer to my question. Will you two get married? I think you ought to."

"Listen, Tracy. I'm not sure that I believe in signing that piece of paper again. I think it stands for an out-dated way of life. Who needs the results of that kind of bargain? The only thing you get out of it is to feel possessed."

"Come on stupid," Tracy said. "What makes you think someone like you will feel possessed just because you're married? I say that if you're going to climb a mountain, and living with someone these days is just that, then you better put your mountain climbing shoes on. If only to keep society from dragging you down.

It's hard enough these days trying to make it with a guy and having a baby. Don't give yourself any extra work. Besides, you better think about Robert. He's not as evolved as you. He wants to feel pinned down and the marriage certificate, or that piece of paper, as you call it, will make him feel just that. Protect yourself baby, protect yourself."

Dreaming: She is standing in the middle of a never-ending line-up of women. She sees her Russian grand-mother being fitted with a yoke upon her back. Methodically, the man places a yoke on each woman's back. Then a noose around each neck. Harriet knows her turn is coming. She silently prays: When the execu-tioner pulls the switch please don't let me remain alive. I can't live with a yoke on my back.

September 1. Sitting on the steps of the new flat. Ner-vously biting her thumb nail.

Harriet wondered how long it would take before one of the moving men made another complaint.

"Listen, Miss. We don't have all day to wait around you know. We've got two other jobs before this day is finished. Is that friend of yours coming with the key or isn't he?"

"I'm terribly sorry. He was supposed to be here at eleven with the keys. I don't know what's holding him up. But I'm sure he'll be here any minute."

"Well, he better be. We can't wait much longer. If he doesn't get here soon we'll just have to move off with your stuff in the van."

"I understand and I do appreciate your waiting around."

Harriet rearranged her body on the steps. What's with Robert anyway? He's done nothing at all to help with this move. He could at least have gotten here on time.

She jumped up. "It's O.K. now. There he is. That's his car."

"A good thing too," the mover grunted.

"Where have you been, Robert? You're an hour late. These men are flipping, and I don't blame them."

"Sorry," Robert said. "I didn't realize how late it was. Anyway here I am."

"I've been sitting on these steps for an hour. Can you realize that?"

Robert fumbled through his pockets.

"What now?" Harriet asked. "Don't tell me you don't have the keys."

"Looks like it," Robert said. "I was sure I took them off the table and put them into my pocket before I left my flat."

"You're really anxious for us to get into this flat together, aren't you?"

"Skip the analytical stuff Harriet, will you?" Robert said. "Don't make a fuss about nothing. All I did was forget the keys."

"Well you better do something about it fast. These movers have had it."

"O.K. O.K. How about that window? I'll climb up on the balcony and try to open it from the outside."

Harriet watched the two movers and Robert trying to wedge the window open. This could be funny if I wasn't furious, she thought. But I am. What the hell was he trying to prove by arriving late, and without the keys? I better cool down and like he says, skip the analytical stuff.

"O.K.," Robert shouted from the balcony. "I can climb in now and open the front door."

Robert strutted out of the flat. "Pretty clever move I thought of, wasn't it? I'll be back in an hour. There's a horse I want to get some money on for the one o'clock race. Bye darling."

I lie still on the table. Wondering where Sally and Tracy are. And Robert. What's taking them so long? Where's the nurse? Or the doctor? Maybe they've forgotten about me. Please. Don't let the contractions start with nobody here. I won't be able to forget about me. The contractions will start any minute to remind me that I'm here. How much worse will the pain get? What time is it? How long have I been in this room? How often do the contractions come? I must remember to ask Sally about that when she comes back. She'll know.

Months ago. Before I was even wearing pregnancy clothes. Sally describing Simon's birth: 'It was simple as pie having Simon. I learned the exercises at Mrs. Walker's class. Practiced a bit at home and toned my muscles up. Bill was with me right through the labor. When things got bad he massaged my neck and legs.'

Is Robert massaging a neck and legs now?

'It was great having Bill there. Really eased the tension. He amused me and helped me through the bad spots. And he was with me the moment Simon was born. I'm sure with Robert there you'll have an easy time. With his sense of humor you'll be laughing the whole time.'

'Everything you touch turns to poison you brat. You can't do anything like normal people do. Can you?'

'You're a good kid but you always have to be different. Don't you, kid?'

I look around the room. Up at the light bulb hanging from the ceiling. Why don't they have a shade on that bulb? At the four white walls. Into the wooden chair next to the small sink. Around the empty room again. Robert isn't here. I lost him. I'm lost. He doesn't know what's happening to me. He's making his scene in London. As if I don't exist. Maybe I won't exist for long. Maybe I'll die here, Robert, and you'll never see me again. I'll die, that's what I'll do. Not of a broken spirit like I wanted to die of these last few months. But here in a New York hospital. In childbirth. Your child.

('She was so tense and nervous and worn out by the time she got to the hospital that there was nothing we could do to save her life, Mr. Felton.')

Then would you be the sweet Robert again? Then would you remember me? Love me?

'Let's get married, darling. It was so great to hear you tell Kathy and Nick about the baby in you. Sort of like announcing our engagement.'

The contractions are starting to gnaw away at me. Oh God, there they go. Where is everybody? Where is anybody? Don't think. Just get through the pain-two-three-four. A new symptom. Pains in my thighs. What next? Terrible pain in my thighs. I'm on a rack being torn apart limb by limb. Must ask the doctor if pains in the thighs are normal. Where's the doctor? What's normal now? Maybe Robert was acting normal and it was me who reacted like a madwoman. Other women would have known how to handle him. I didn't want to handle him.

'Robert wants to feel pinned down and the marriage certificate will make him feel just that.'

'I've told you before, Tracy. I don't want to pin any-one down. I haven't spent over two years learning to trust Robert and myself enough to choose to live together all for the sake of pinning him down. I want us to be together because we want to be.'

'Protect yourself, baby. Protect yourself.'

It's my fault for not acting like he wanted me to. Maybe it's my fault for not pretending. I should have pretended that I didn't notice how frightened he was. How oppressively he behaved. How frightened I became. Robert got what he wanted after all. A scared-to-death me. Maybe I should have ignored him like he ignored me. I never should have let Robert know that I really loved him. He treated me better when he wasn't sure.

'I love you, Harriet. Really love you. It's the first time in my life that I haven't felt trapped with a woman. Haven't felt the need to prove that I'm independent. It's because of you, darling. I know that you want me to feel free and alive. And I know that's what you want for yourself. It's so easy loving you.'

'Stop this bloody inquisition will you? I don't know why I've come home at five in the morning. I feel trapped in this flat with you. That's what I feel. Trapped and gone off you.'

Shut up. Stop it and just get through this pain. It has to stop sometime. Very soon.

This is the worst part. In the heart of the whirling wave. Being tossed about. Endlessly. Nothing I can do about it but give myself up to the ferocious turmoil of the water. And breathe-two-three-four-five-six. There. It's over. And I'm not drowned. I'm on the calm surface again. Until the next wave attacks. And it will. But for this minute I'm alive. Alone in this room.

Waiting to hear the sound of Ben's latch key. Before feeling safe enough for sleeping. Always waiting for Ben to change my mood. To make me feel safe. To make me feel alive.

'Come on, kid. We'll go to the garage to get the car. Come on, kid. I'll take you to the races with me today. Stay out of school today, kid, and your old man will take you with him to the clothing showroom. It's Friday, and I'm going to do some buying. Don't tell your mother, kid, but we'll go to a night club tonight. The Copa or the Latin Quarter. They've got some beautiful dolls at the Latin Quarter. So get dressed up in your best.'

'Say, Franny. This kid of mine is something isn't she? She's certainly a chip off her daddy's block. Looks like my mother, you know. Just like our side of the family. Nothing to do with Jeannie or her family. Go on, kid. Give us a dance. She dances like a queen. Don't forget, kid. Don't tell your mother about that show we saw at the Copa. She'll start screaming about how I never take her out anywhere.'

'O.K. Ben. I won't.' Panicking. In cahoots with Ben. But it's awful being treated like Jeannie. I'll be different.

Then no man will treat me like that. But what if it's Ben's fault? My life will be different. Very different. Dear God please make my mommy and daddy stop fighting and screaming and yelling at each other. Star light star bright first star I see tonight I wish I may I wish I might have the wish I wish tonight: Please make my mommy and daddy be nice to each other and make my mommy stop yelling at me all the time and make Ben stay home more. Thank you and I'll be a good girl. I promise.

Lying in bed beside Harvey. Late at night. 'Whose fault is it that they yell and hate each other so much?'

'His, stupid. He treats her like dirt. Never takes her anywhere. Stays out all night and makes her beg for money.'

'Yes, Harvey. That's true. But what about her? She's always complaining and always screaming and picking on everyone. Everything he likes to do she screams about.'

'You bum. It's clear you've just been to the races. I can smell the horses on you. Can't you ever get home at a decent hour? I'm damn tired of serving dinner to you every night at eleven.'

Feeling sorry for Jeannie. 'Listen, Jeannie. If you don't want to serve dinner so late why do you? Let him get his own and then maybe he'll stop coming in so late.'

'What do you know about anything? All you have to

do is give him one of your smiles and you get anything you want from him. You're a spoiled brat, that's what you are. But he'll learn one of these days. One of these days he'll suffer for spoiling you. When you end up in the gutter somewhere. Or become a whore like the tramps he hangs around with.'

And from Harvey: 'Of course he likes you and treats you great. Gives you money and everything. That's because you'd do anything for him. Kiss his feet if he asked you to. Me. I'd rather starve than go begging from him. He stinks.'

Trying. Always trying to figure it out. Logically. It's true he's not nice to Jeannie, but she's so nasty.

'Can I have my fifty cents, Ben? It's Saturday. The day for my allowance.'

'O.K. kid. Give me a little dance first. Are you sure I didn't give you your money yesterday?'

'You know you didn't, Ben. You're just teasing me.'

'O.K. Here it is.'

Maybe I would do anything to please him. Maybe Harvey is right. But I like him. I love my daddy. If he were here more she wouldn't be able to yell and scream at me so much. Where is he? When is he coming home?

In the white dress I made in sewing class. Jeannie talking to me: 'Well you see how much he cares for you. Doesn't even come to his own daughter's public school graduation. All the other fathers were there. His

75

business and pleasure come first. That's how much he cares about you. He was probably at the race track. Or out with one of his women. But I came. Didn't I? Even with all I have to do.'

I wonder what she has to do.

'I'm the mother who's supposed to be so terrible. I'm the only one who gives a damn about you and don't you forget it. I've brought you kids up alone. Diapers and caring about kids is one thing he's run away from like the plague. Then he gets all the love from you. Well, one day you'll learn. What a good mother I am.'

Never mentioning to Ben about his not being there at the P.S. 82 graduation ceremonies. Never telling about the hole in my stomach and how I stopped breathing for a second when I spotted Jeannie's face in the audience. Surrounded by two strangers. Other people's fathers. Telling myself over and over and over how he works and can't stay away from work just because his daughter is graduating.

'One day when you have your own kids then you'll see what it's like bringing up kids with a man like your father. Then you'll know what a good mother I've been. Wait till you have your own kids. Then you'll see.'

This is having a kid and the pain is starting again-two-three-four. They don't cut a hole in your stomach and take the baby out. How long did I believe that?

Out-two-three-four. Until I was eleven-twelve-thirteen. I don't remember-two-three-four.

I open my eyes. For the pain that travels downhill before the agonizing climb up again.

I see Tracy and Sally enter the room. I smile to them through the breathing. And remember Sally's words: 'Concentrate on yourself. This is your show. Forget about the rest of the world and what they're up to.'

They'll understand. They'll know I'm in pain. It's all right. They won't leave me alone again. Soon this century of a round will be over. Then I can talk to them.

Sally comes over to me. She takes my hand and squeezes concern into it. "That's good," she says. "Now keep it high on your chest. Good. Very good."

Out-two-three-four-five-six-seven-finished.

I force out an expression of recognition.

"I've been trying to remember what you said, Sally. To concentrate on myself. That's why I didn't stop when you came into the room. They're over now. They've stopped. Where have you been?"

"We've just come from the Bursar's Office," Tracy says. "Can you imagine? I don't believe this city. They told us that we had to put down a one hundred dollar deposit so that you could stay here. I told them that I didn't exactly take the time to think about bringing money with me when you started bleeding and I had to call the hospital and get you ready to go. God knows what they would have done if I didn't happen to have my check book on me. Throw us all out into the street or something, I guess. But I told them off all right. Before I gave them the check."

"Is it all right now?" I ask. "Is it settled now?"

"Yes. It's all right now. It's all taken care of. Just don't you think about it," Tracy says. "The financial end is finished for now."

Pleading: 'Listen, Ben. It's you who pays. So if you say I can go to camp this summer then she'll have to let me go. Please Ben. I want to go away so badly. I'm fourteen and I've never been away before. Harvey goes to summer camp all the time. Besides, Ben. I don't know why she wants me around here with her. All she does is pick on me. You know that. Please, Ben. Please sign me up. And this camp is cheaper than others. It's a kind of work camp, Ben. You can work on a farm if you want to in the morning. But in the afternoon you're under their supervision. And Ellen, my best friend, she's going. And Jeannie knows her parents. Tell her to call them up. Anything, Ben. But please help me to go. To get away from here. At least for this summer.'

'O.K. kid. I'll see what I can do.'

"Is everything all right?" Sally asks.

"It seems as if the contractions are coming so much

more often now," I answer. "How often do they come? Can you tell me that."

"As time goes on they'll come at closer intervals," Sally says. "I don't know how often they've been coming for you. But I'll time the next two. We can get an idea that way."

"Thanks, Sally. And there's something else."

Something else, something else? What was it? Oh yes.

"I'm beginning to get terrible pains in my thighs along with the contractions."

"That's normal. It's because of the pressure being put on them when your womb contracts. It might begin to happen in the base of your spine too. Don't worry. If it gets too bad then Tracy and I can massage it where it hurts."

"Of course," Tracy says. "Just let us know where the pain is. And we'll massage it."

Tracy sits down on one side of me. Sally on the other. Each of them takes a sweaty hand.

I look at them. I see them looking at a lost puppy I once saw. The one I wanted to bring home but knew I couldn't.

"Next time," Tracy says, "it will be Robert holding your hand."

There was a Robert who held my hand. There was a Robert who ignored my hand when I begged him to take it. He pushed it away as if it were poison. There were two Roberts. If Robert were two separate men I could understand. I can't fit the two together. I must have done something to make him change. I did something. I must be going mad. Because I wish the pains would start again. I'd have to concentrate on them. And stop trying to figure out what I did and what happened to make Robert split in two. I could stop thinking about Robert. If the pains started I could stop. Stop!

September 25. Arranging furniture. In the living room.

Harriet and Sue shoved the bookcase into the corner near the window.

"That must be Robert coming home," Harriet said. "I hear his footsteps in the hall."

"Good," Sue said. "Now we'll get some man power into this business. You shouldn't be pushing heavy things around anyway."

"Come on, Sue. Can you see me acting the part of the helpless, pregnant woman?"

Robert entered the living room. He looked around as if he was on some strange planet. "Another bookcase, Harriet? And what's that? Not another mirror. Looks like the little woman has been on a shopping spree. When did all this stuff arrive?"

Harriet puffed up the pillow on the couch. "This afternoon."

"Well, it looks like you plan on making this flat into a library. Why don't you sell all those books of yours or throw them into the garbage? That's what I'd do if they were mine. What do we need them all over the place for? Show?"

"Since when, Mr. Oxford, are you so anti-books?" Sue asked.

"I just don't feel like living in a library, that's all."

Dreaming: Of being thrown out of the house by her mother. She runs to her book shelves. Throws one book after another into a large wooden box. Quickly. Before Jeannie takes over the house. Jeannie stands there. Screaming: 'All those books you read. What the hell good do they do you but turn you into a communist believer in free love? Give you a whole lot of fancy ideas that don't mean a damn out in the world. That's where you have to live you know. In the world. Just like everybody else. You're no better than any other woman.' Harriet rushes out into the street. Looking desperately for her baby. She stares at the man opening the lid of a garbage bin. He smiles smugly at her. 'I knew I'd find your baby in the garbage bin. That's where it comes from. The dirty garbage bin.'

October 2. Drinking brandies at the bar. During the intermission of the Merce Cunningham Group.

Harriet said, "Cunningham has really got his group and ideas shaped up since I last saw them in New York. That must have been at least six years ago."

"They are good," Robert answered. "But the standard of dancing technique is pretty low. Compared with ballet standards."

"That doesn't bother me. The ideas explored are so much more penetrating than those airy fairy ballet themes."

"We better go back," Robert said. "I think we're going to be late getting to our seats."

"Would you mind standing in the back until this ballet is finished?" the usher requested. "It will be on for about seven minutes."

Standing in the back of the auditorium. Harriet

tapped Robert on the shoulder. "I feel a bit faint. Like I better get some air."

Concentrating on the stage, he replied, "This dance won't last much longer. Try not to think about it."

Harriet observed herself standing there. Leaning lightly on Robert. Unable to move. I ought to get out of here with or without Robert, she thought. If I don't I'm going to faint. How the hell can he be so insensitive? Acting as if I'm not here. No less in pain.

The lights and applause flashed on.

"Robert, I'm going to faint. Help me out of here, quickly."

"O.K. Come on."

He seated her in the lobby. "I'll go and see if I can get you some water."

Harriet waited. It's so stupid of me. I'm embarrassed in front of these theater-goers. Like that time Robert kept me waiting for an hour in that restaurant a few years ago. Humiliated in front of the hat check girl. Clear to her that somebody was standing me up. Robert coming in with that excuse about not being able to find a parking space for his car. Saying he'd be back in five minutes when he finished parking. Waiting another half hour. Getting more and more embarrassed and furious. Leaving the restaurant. Robert standing on the street corner kissing a girl. The one he had to get rid of before joining me in the restaurant. How did I ever manage to get over that scene? I swore I'd never see him again. I got a terrible cold the next day.

Robert stood in front of her. "Here's some water, darling. And an aspirin. The usher had some on him. Are you feeling better?"

"Yes, I am. The lobby air is what I really needed."

"Good. I'll be right back. You better sit there until the next ballet. I'm just going to say hello to Danny."

Harriet watched Robert. Chatting gaily with Danny. Then Louise. He took out his address book and scribbled Louise's sounds into it.

The scene with Peter rushed through Harriet's head. Peter asking: 'Why do you look so surprised, Harriet? So my wife's in the hospital having a baby and I come on with you. You're a big girl. A sophisticated lady.'

Robert returned. "Do you feel better now? You look a lot better."

"Yes. I'm all right. How's Louise? What's she doing these days?"

"Fine. She's fine. She's singing at Ronnie's Club. I think I'll go see her next week."

Dreaming: Of watching Louise dancing with a man. Louise moves her pregnant belly to the rhythm of the music. The man pulls her closer and closer. He becomes the caricature of the dirty old lech. Poor Louise,

Harriet thinks. I'll go and dance with her. I'll dance with her and make her feel better. He's making her feel so dirty.

Of entering a restaurant. Robert sits doing the *Times'* crossword puzzle. He looks at her and returns to his puzzle. 'Why do you pretend not to recognize me?' she asks. 'Why do you act as if I'm not here? Why do you turn your back on me?' 'Don't be silly, baby,' Robert says. 'I didn't know it was you who just came in. I didn't see you.' 'Never mind,' she says. 'Just give me the keys to the car. I want to go for a drive.' Tracy appears outside the restaurant. 'You are stupid,' she says. 'Really stupid. I have a friend who doesn't drive. So her husband has to take her everywhere. Shopping and all over. She's not so dumb for not learning how to drive. Gets everything done for her that way.' Harriet gets into the car. Starts driving. She turns the wheel to make a right turn. The car swerves left.

October 10. Going to a private showing at the Drian Gallery.

Sue and Harriet waited for Robert to pull the car around to the front of the house.

"What's with Robert?" Sue asked. "He's acting very

peculiar. As if he can't stand being inside the flat for more than a minute. And he's so strange with you. Almost as if he's trying to make it appear like he doesn't care about you, or what you feel like doing. I've never seen him like that before. And he's a bad actor. Off stage, that is. He's behaving like a little boy."

"This performance has been going on since we moved into the flat together. He's been acting like a child all right. And he's cast me as the apron string strangler. So every act of his is to make me less and less secure and more and more concentrated on what his next bit will be. I feel like an intruding house guest in my own flat. Every time I try to talk to him about it he reacts as if he doesn't know what I'm talking about. Maybe he doesn't. These aren't exactly the best conditions for me now. I haven't been able to concentrate long enough to get down to my book."

Entering the gallery.

Robert made a bee line for the crowd.

Harriet tried to calm herself. Nothing strange about what Robert's doing. Robert is often like that. Likes to be on his own in a room filled with people. For that matter, so do I. Stop feeling hurt, stupid. Find a familiar face.

"Hello, John," she said. "How are you?"

"Great, and you? I say. You're pregnant. And lovely with it. You look beautiful. You ought to be having babies all the time. It suits you."

Harriet smiled. "Thanks. How's the photography going? I saw your last series in *Nova*. They were great."

John continued talking. She repeated orders to herself: That's right. Smile and talk and make like you're listening. And don't fall apart. Be interested in the outside. Forget about how you feel. Keep talking and smiling and talking. Why is Robert pretending that I'm not here? That I've got nothing to do with him? I feel like I'm not here. Like I'm going to disappear. I better get out of here.

Robert and a tall dark-haired girl appeared in front of Harriet.

"Harriet, this is Margaret Garrin," Robert said. "We're going over to the pub next door for a drink. Do you want to come?"

"No thanks. I'd like to go home now. It's too hot and stuffy in here for me. I've had enough."

"Oh, come on, Harriet. It's the first night in a long time that I feel any good. Come along with us to the pub."

He's performing a ritual, she thought. It's called politeness. He's treating me like a casual acquaintance. I don't want him to go. I want him to take me home.

"No, Robert," she said. "But you go."

She waited for his reaction.

"O.K. I feel good tonight."

"Would you just get me a cab before you go?"

She felt that it wasn't for her that Robert hailed the cab. He opened the door of the taxi. Placed a pound note into her hand, and told the driver the address.

"Are you sure you don't want to come with us?" he asked again.

"Yes. I'm going home."

Driving home. Better to be alone. Better to feel like this than watch Robert come on with that chick. Maybe he's not coming on with her at all. Maybe I'm over sensitive now. Possessive and acting like a jealous bitch. Could it be my fault that he's acting this way? Spending less and less time with me since we moved into the flat together. Like he can't be with me alone any more. What should I do to make him feel better? He's changed. I'm to blame. Somewhere. He did choose this scene. He did want it, ask for it, plan it. Now he acts as if I'm the plague. Don't exaggerate everything. It's just that he felt like being with people. Nothing wrong with that. It's just that I'm feeling abandoned. And Robert's nervous. Try and understand him.

Dreaming: Of flying. Quietly. Slowly. Towards Robert from behind him. Of strangling him from behind his back. Harriet hesitates with fear. What would happen if Robert should turn around and see my intention before I finish murdering him? It becomes clear. He'll simply touch a vulnerable part of me. Any vulnerable part. Even a knee. And then I'll suffer in agonizing pain. Far more pain than Robert. I'll forget the whole idea of murder before he finds out my thoughts. If he knows, he'll kill me. Or leave me unprotected. With this baby in me.

Waking in a sweat.

Harriet saw Robert standing at the bedroom door.

He switched on the overhead light and stared blankly at her.

"Why aren't you sleeping? It's three in the morning. You look awful. Have you been lying here crying?"

"I'm not crying. I'm not crying now. But I've been having nightmares. I've been feeling like I'm going mad. I know you just wanted to be with people tonight, but I keep feeling that you don't want to be with me. I know that's not true but I can't get it out of my mind. Did you have a nice time?"

"Not bad. Not bad at all."

"Forgive me for all this, Robert. I am acting like you said. Like a silly little woman. Forgive me and come

to bed. Come to bed and hold me. Hold me, Robert. I
need you to hold me."

Roughly moving into her. "You see, my darling. Even
intellectuals need fucking, don't they? I'm big in you,
aren't I? Really big. I can feel myself very high up
into you. I'm big. Aren't I?"

"Yes, Robert. You're very big in me."

And to herself: You're so big, you're God. Jesus
Christ. Rhett Butler. Burt Lancaster. Anyone you want
to be, but hold me. Hold me until I come. God. How
did I get here? Hating him and begging him to love
me in the same breath. How did I get here?

After coming. Stillness. Frightened of opening her
eyes. Like after masturbating. Afraid of the sight of the
room.

"Better get some sleep now," he said. "I've got to
get up early for a rehearsal. To earn for all of this."

Dreaming: Of a Sunday drive in the car with Ben.
A little girl lies in the road in front of their moving
car. Ben keeps driving. Doesn't even slow down. Harriet knows he's going to run over her. She knows
the little girl won't move out of the way. Wondering why she doesn't tell Ben to stop. That he's

about to wound the little girl. She can't. She sits there paralyzed. Unable to tell Ben to stop. She just watches him ride over the child and wound her hand. Her right hand.

Of walking gaily along the street with Ben. Towards a restaurant and a night out together. Suddenly, Ben turns to her. Shoves a five dollar note into her hand. 'Sorry, kid. I can't make it now but here's five dollars instead.' Harriet screams: 'I don't want the money. I want to be with you. I want you to be with me. I don't want the money.' Screaming and vomiting. 'I don't want the money. I want to be with you.'

October 27. Lying in bed.

Harriet watched the hand of the clock move from twenty-six-minutes-to-four to twenty-five-minutes-to-four. She changed position from right side to left. Knowing that there was no comfortable posture. No direction to move into for relief.

I must ask Doctor Chander for some sleeping pills. It's not good for the baby if I don't sleep. Robert's never done this before. Stayed out all night. He did say he'd be home after dinner with Jeff. 'Home at midnight,' he said. It can't be that he's really going to stay out all night. Robert's not like that. He's probably had an accident. That's it. He's in trouble and here I am worrying about what he's up to. Stop kidding yourself. He's out. Coming on with some chick. Now. I'm the girl he's out with tonight. Or him. For thinking that thought I must be punished. Bend down and touch the floor with your hands. Pull up your skirt but leave your panties on. Make Robert say, 'I'm going to beat you on the behind. Beat you with a cane. A black cane. Then I'll enter you from behind. Take you like a dog.' Now I'll be Robert. I have a big prick instead of this big belly. And I'm shoving it into a warm cunt. Just a little more and I'll come. My hand is getting tired. Don't stop. Go on. Just a bit more. There. Maybe I can sleep now. Sleep deeply. Not be awake when Robert comes home. When he climbs into bed next to me.

Dreaming: Of crying into space: 'I will die if I make this baby. The baby won't be still-born. But I will die if I create a baby.'

Of looking at a newborn baby: 'What a pretty little baby,' Harriet says to the woman. 'What a beautiful baby. Let me hold it.' Horrified by what she sees, she drops the child. Drops the pretty little girl who has a penis growing out of her eye.

Doctor Parker enters the room. He sees Tracy wiping the sweat from my forehead. Sally rubbing my thighs and telling me not to talk.

"Get all the rest you can between contractions," she says.

Doctor Parker speaks: "You ladies are certainly making my job easy tonight. There isn't much for me to do here with you two around."

Sally and Tracy continue their rituals. Their focus

leaves me for a second. To acknowledge Doctor Parker's presence.

"And you, Harriet," Doctor Parker continues, "you certainly are a good patient. I wish all the women could be like you. How are you feeling?"

"I'm tired. Very tired. The contractions are getting worse and worse. And they're coming so often. I'm tired."

"We could give you an injection to ease the pain a bit. But that would slow the baby's trip down. And it will take longer that way. Especially as your baby is smaller than usual. And without much strength to help its journey."

The baby is small. It can't help itself. But do I have the energy to get through this? I can't take much more. I'm as crippled and powerless as my baby. He doesn't seem to want to give me an injection. What's his reason? Maybe a drug would be harmful to the baby.

I say, "I'll try and do without a drug for a while. For as long as I can."

"That's good. Now let's have another look at you."

"She's getting bad pains in her spine now," Tracy says.

"That's fairly normal but I'll have a look at it anyway," Doctor Parker says. "Turn over on your stomach now. As much as you can without having it hurt you."

'Now I won't really hurt you, Harriet.' Uncle Sam

talking in a semiwhisper: 'It's only a game we're going to play.'

'What kind of a game? I want to know the rules.'

Uncle Sam telling me: 'We'll just pretend that you've been a bad girl. Now turn over onto your stomach and I'll punish you for being naughty. I'll spank you on your little round behind.'

It's a game. I'm a very naughty nine-year-old and that's why he's spanking me. With his hand. I feel him hit me. Not very hard. And before each not very hard hit I feel a gentle caressing hand. Rubbing my behind. That's a different feeling. A very different feeling. It must be part of the game. That must be why I'm naughty. Because I get a funny feeling when he caresses my behind, in between those just pretend spanks. Such a funny feeling. I mustn't tell anybody about that funny feeling. Or ever think about that funny feeling. Don't dare tell. But there's something funny about Uncle Sam. That other time. When I was six. When he took me into the basement. Took it out and told me to play with it. 'Pat it and stroke it and touch it all over.' Remembering to forget the whole thing. How frightened I was of what he'd take out next if I didn't play with it. And you're not supposed to see that part of men so I won't tell anybody. After that. Uncle Sam sitting at family dinners, eating chicken soup like everyone else. Me looking at him and asking him to pass the salt, please. Not telling. Anybody.

Jeannie always saying, 'It's such a shame that your aunt doesn't have any children. Your Uncle Sam would have been such a good father. Not like that bum of a husband I married.'

Not telling anybody. They'd kill me if they knew what nice Uncle Sam made me do. But there wasn't any funny feeling that time in the basement. Not like in this game. There's that funny feeling again. It comes every time his hand caresses my bottom. Now just forget that feeling. The one I'm beginning to get now when he hits me lightly. Forget it. Quick.

Doctor Parker says, "Your back is all right, Harriet. You can turn around again. You're just having the usual pains caused by the pressure of contractions."

"Give me your hand now, please. I'm going to check your pulse."

That funny feeling again. Holding hands with Martin at summer camp. Underneath the oak tree on the top of the flower-covered hill. Noting the difference. His hand is black. Mine is white.

Dear Diary: Tonight as Martin and I held hands I realized how much fuss people make over the most stupid things. How wrong it is that so many people would get mad about Martin and me. Just because his hand is black and mine is white. I will hide you, Dear

Diary, when I get home after the summer so that Jeannie can't read you. I like Martin. He is sweet and gentle. Tonight I let him kiss me good night. I will be his girl friend from now on. Not George's any more. I like square dancing with George, but I like Martin better. His mother is the nurse here.

"That's fine," Doctor Parker says. "Your pulse is fine."

He looks first at Sally, then at Tracy. "Perhaps you two ladies would like to go and have a cup of coffee or something now. You both must be pretty exhausted."

"All right," Tracy says. "We are sort of tired."

She gets up from her chair. Squeezes my hand and says, "We'll be back soon. Keep calm. Everything's O.K."

I catch a glimpse of their faces as they get up to leave. Almost featureless with exhaustion. For the first time I think about them.

They've been with me for hours. Never missing a contraction. Somehow letting me know they're here every time the pain starts. Resting their heads on the table only when my pain stops.

"Now the nurse is going to insert an instrument into your vagina," Doctor Parker says. "To hold it open so that I can see how things are inside of you."

'Now Ben. Now you can see what goes on inside her. What kind of filth is in that head of hers. And she's only fourteen. Already she has no respect for society and its rules. I told you not to send her to that communist camp. That nothing but trouble would come from it. Well. Just look at this. I found her diary today. Proof. Of the kinds of thoughts she thinks. That those of us who respect the rules of society are the crazy ones. And the kinds of things she's up to. Kissing niggers and God knows what else. Someone better beat some sense into her before it's too late. For all we know she's pregnant with a black baby. See how you'll like that. She's got no sense of decency and it's because of you. She ought to be locked up. Until she learns how to behave like other girls. Other decent girls.'

"Stop it. Stop it please, Doctor Parker. I'm getting the contractions again."

"All right, Harriet. We'll stop for the moment. You go ahead and do the breathing. We'll wait until they're over before we continue to examine you."

Go on. Breathe. They've got to stop and I've got to get through them. Nothing I can do to stop them. Just endure it and get through these pains. They'll stop in a while. You know that by now. They always stop. Before starting again. Now out. Now in. I've lost count. Never mind. They're subsiding-four-five-six.

"You're doing fine," Doctor Parker says.

I feel his hand ploughing further and further up into me.

"Everything is quite normal in here," he says.

'You're not normal. That's what it is. You're just not normal. Any normal girl of your age wouldn't be up to the filth that you are. I know you're still seeing him. Well let me tell you this. I'll break every bone in your body if I find out that you ever see him again. You're not going to any more of those parties where any of those bums from that free love camp go. Do you hear? I'll kill you if you see that nigger again. You tell her, Ben. She won't listen to anything I say. Isn't her diary proof enough? Of the way she thinks. Of how her filthy fourteen-year-old mind works. You can read can't you? Well read what she's written. Then you'll see what kind of a daughter you've raised. A slut. A whore. That's what she is. Well, what are you going to do about it? Stand around and let it happen? Watch her grow up and have black babies? Is that what you're going to do? Well you can't laugh this away like you do everything else she does. She's your daughter as well you know and she's disgraced us. What if your mother knew about her disgusting behavior. Or your sisters? How would you feel about that? It's all here. On these pages of her diary. Right here in front of your nose. In black and white. Right here for you to see. You've got a nigger-lover for a daughter. What are you going to do about it? A nigger-lover and a sex maniac.'

Doctor Parker's hand gently eases itself out of me. "I'm not hurting you, am I?" he asks.

"No."

Mike asking: 'What's the matter? Am I hurting you? Why are you crying, pretty one? Tell me. Why are you crying?'

'Because I was a virgin until now. Because I had never done this before.'

'My God. Why didn't you tell me? I never would have made love to you if I'd known that. I don't get my kicks that way. Why didn't you tell me?'

'I thought you knew.'

'No. I didn't know. Did I hurt you?'

'No. It's not that. You didn't hurt me. But I shouldn't have done it. I shouldn't have done it.'

'Well, it's all over now. Don't cry. I'll get up in a minute and make us some coffee.'

On the train back to the university. Thinking about how it would be all right now to make love with Tom. Now that I've had an affair with a total stranger. A man I met in the library. Whom I only had dinner with once. Who was a complete stranger to me. Surely it's all right now to do it with Tom. He's my boy friend. And I like him. Besides. He's tired of my saying no all the time. I'm nineteen. That's not so young. In a few hours I'll be in Tom's arms. Thanks to that stranger.

Six months later. The boils coming back again. For the first time in five years.

'And those boils, Ben? What do you think they're about? Well, I'll tell you. They're from all that contact with that nigger. She never had them before this summer and that sex mad commie camp. Now what are you going to do about her? *Your* daughter.'

"There, Harriet. I'm done examining you now. You're doing quite well. The baby is making its trip just as it should be. Just a bit slower than usual. But other than the extra length of time and work for you in labor, it seems as if all is well."

I'm getting the contractions again. Breathe. In-two-three-four. Out-two-three-four. God. I don't believe it. The ridiculousness of it all. I've got a kink in my right leg along with these contractions. What next?

"My leg. There's a terrible cramp in my right leg, Doctor Parker. Like when you're swimming. It hurts. Terribly."

Out-two-three-four. Knowing Jeannie is standing in the wet sand. So she can see me. I'll pretend I'm drowning. That I've got a cramp in my leg. Staying under water with my hands waving madly above the surface. The lifeguard taking my game seriously. Rushing in and carrying me out.

'I was only joking. Only playing. I didn't think you'd

see. I was only teasing my mother by pretending I was drowning.'

'Those kind of jokes aren't funny, little girl.'

Jeannie yelling at me. Even before she knew it was a game. Not worried. Like I hoped. Just screaming at me at the top of her lungs. 'Who do you think you are, you brat? Going out so far. If I catch you doing that again you'll spend the rest of the summer out of the water, you no good brat.'

Wishing I had really drowned. Always wishing. Never expecting. Any caring about me from Jeannie. Or any other woman.

'Will Harriet Battenberg please come to the front of the class. I want her to read her essay on last week's bombing of Pearl Harbor.'

Petrified with fear. I never should have written what I did in that essay. I never should have written how awful I think war is. Any war, anywhere. Now Mrs. Newman is angry with me. She's going to show the whole class how stupid I am. Make me read my essay and then get angry at me for writing such a stupid paper.

Holding the blue lined, yellow essay paper in my shaking hand. Reading to the class: 'From what I have already said in this essay you can now understand how sick I feel about wars and hundreds of innocent people dying.'

Mrs. Newman telling me to sit down, and saying: 'Now class. I had Harriet read her essay because I think it is the best one turned in to me. It's beautifully written and I think the ideas are worth discussing during this next half hour. Johnny. What did you feel about Harriet's ideas?'

Amazed in my wooden seat. And thrilled. She liked it. She said it was the best essay in the class. I love her. I love Mrs. Newman. I'll work so hard this term. She'll see. She'll see how good I am. And smart. I love her and one day I'll do something. Something that will make her proud of me. She liked my essay. She likes me.

Doctor Parker works at rubbing away my cramp. His hands move gently. Back and forth around my calf.

"There. How does it feel now? Better?"

"Yes. It's going away. But please don't stop rubbing yet. The cramp is still there."

Which will stop first? The pain in my leg or the contractions?

For a split second I am outside myself. Laughing at the girl with a cramp in her leg during contractions. And inside myself. Crying to the rhythm of the pain-two-three-four.

"Is your cramp gone now?" Doctor Parker asks.

"Yes. Thank you for rubbing it."

"Your right leg must be all tied up. I'll massage the

entire leg for you now. Get the circulation going so the cramp doesn't come back."

'Well. What are you going to do about her? It's out of my hands but I tell you that you're in for a long line of messy trouble from her if you don't knock some common sense into her. Do you hear me, Ben?'

Getting sense knocked in. All thought and feeling knocked out. Replaced by shock. Ben's arms swinging away at my face-legs-thighs-stomach-breasts. I must cover my breasts. Someone's hands beating me about until I fall onto the green carpet in the living room. Crumpled up on the green carpet. I can't protest because this isn't happening to me. This maniac beating me up can't be Ben. But cover your breasts. He's going to kill me if he doesn't stop. I can't resist this beating because it isn't happening. Not to me. Ben's arms flapping madly. As if his life depended on killing me. Ben isn't doing this to me. Not the Ben who loves me. The Ben who never hit me before. Not in my whole life. The Ben who makes me laugh. Makes life bearable in this mad house. The Ben who takes me to night clubs and dances with me as if we'd been born dancing together. *The* Ben. Watch out at least for your breasts. Cover your breasts with your hands. It doesn't really hurt. None of it. Maybe he'll stop before he kills me. A thus across the face forces out the words: 'Stop. Stop it, Ben.'

"Am I hurting you, Harriet," Doctor Parker asks.

"No. No. My leg feels much better now. Thank you."

Jeannie screaming: 'Stop, Ben. Stop it already. You'll kill her.'

"Well then. I'll leave you here now. Your friends will be back soon."

Doctor Parker walks out of the room. He leaves the door open.

I hear a wailing-screaming-crying sound.

It must be another woman in labor. Down the hall. Her cries are coming closer. She probably got out of bed and she's wandering down the hall. Looking for a doctor or someone to moan into. It must be that a lot of women go through these contractions without any technique to help them. No breathing exercises to concentrate on. They've never been taught. All they do is suffer. They have no technique for easing the pain. They don't even know what's happening to them. Just suffering in a fog of pain. Uselessly. Like they can't do anything to help themselves. As if anyone could do anything for them at this time. Well, they can't help themselves if they're not taught how to. Childbirth classes should be compulsory. Thank God for Sally. I have a technique. And there are my pains again. So use that technique. Don't let the pain get on top of you. Stay with it. Exert an influence over it-two-three-four. Concentrate on yourself-two-three-four. Don't

106

cup of coffee to Mrs. Williams and one to Harriet. Walked over to the cupboard and flung the doors open. Then slammed them closed. He glued his eyes to the floor as if searching for something lost. He started pacing. Back and forth, between cupboard and chair, like a caged animal.

Harriet steadied her voice to speak.

"Are you looking for something, Robert?"

"Yes. The hanger. I'm sure I saw it here. I know I saw it here. Where is it?"

"It's probably in the closet. Where Margaret would put a hanger when she cleaned this room."

He continued to march. Back and forth. His eyes fixed on the carpet. He grunted as he ran his hands through his hair in despair.

He's really going round the bend, she thought. And I'm afraid that I'm going with him.

Rushing into the bathroom. Turning on the bath water.

Harriet hoped to calm down.

Robert entered the bathroom. "Now that you're massaged what do you feel like doing today?"

"I don't know."

"Do you want to go out later?"

pregnant woman should be just as relaxed as possible. Better for the baby that way."

Harriet turned towards the bedroom door. Robert stood there gazing at Mrs. Williams caressing Harriet's shoulders.

"Where are the telephone books?" he asked. "I can't find them anywhere."

"Where they usually are," she replied. "In the top drawer of the chest, near the telephone."

"Oh." He left the room and slammed the door.

Harriet tried to concentrate on relaxing. "There's going to be a scene with Robert," she thought. Her muscles tensed. "I can feel it. Why? It can't be that he's gotten to the point where he can't stand to see anyone give me the slightest bit of attention."

Robert came back into the room. He flipped loudly through the telephone book. Threw it down onto the floor and left.

"Is there something annoying him this morning?" Mrs. Williams asked. "He's acting very peculiar."

"I don't know, Mrs. Williams. I don't know."

She thought: I don't know any more. This has become his normal behavior around here. I'd think I was going mad if Mrs. Williams hadn't commented that his behavior is peculiar. I needed her to tell me that it's not just my imagination.

Robert came back into the room again. He handed a

panic. Know what's happening and keep breathing. Know the cycle of the pain. Know its rhythm inside-out. Know when it begins and when it will end. Understand.

November 11. Relaxing to the rhythm of Mrs. Williams' hands.

Harriet felt the area from neck to shoulders change from stone to flesh.

"How does that feel?" Mrs. Williams asked.

"It hurts a bit while you're doing it. I've been so tense all week. But I know it will feel better tomorrow. It always does after you've massaged me."

"You should try not to get so tense, you know. A

"No. I don't know what my plans are but I don't want to go out with you."

"What's provoking you now? Is it because I came in at four this morning?"

"No. At this point that's the least of it. What was that scene you just pulled with Mrs. Williams? Barging into the room. Asking where telephone books are. Dropping them on the floor and ending in that hanger-hunt routine. I've got to the point where I don't believe what I see any more. I'd think I was making it all up if Mrs. Williams hadn't commented on your peculiar behavior, as she so mildly put it."

"That fat cow. What right does she have to say anything against me?" he screamed. His face contorted with rage. "You should have told her off for saying one word against me. Didn't I bring that fat cow a cup of coffee?"

He really does believe that the women have a conspiracy against him, she thought.

"Never mind that fat cow and all that," she said. "We've got to discuss stopping this madness, somehow. I can't cope with the role you're casting me into. I don't know how to get out of it, but I can't live with it."

"Role casting," he shouted. "What are you talking about? You're mad. You're all mad. It's all a conspiracy to make me lose my head. It's madness, madness. That's what it is. For years now you've been trying to change my head. It's a conspiracy. You're trying to make me mad. What do you want from me? Stop trying to make me mad. And stop trying to discuss everything. That's all you ever want to do. Can't you just let things be, instead of making a scene about every little thing."

Sobbing into the stuffed arm of the chair.

What's going to happen to me? And this baby? I wish I were dead. Really dead. I'll try to sleep. All I want is oblivion.

She put her thumb into her mouth and started to suck.

Dreaming: Of sitting in a car. The woman next to her says, 'We've got to go now. The prison attendants are waiting.' Harriet pleads: 'Please wait just a few more moments. I'm prepared to go to your prison. I want to go. But I know Robert will come to say good-bye. He'll be here soon. I know he will.'

In the department store the woman is transformed into a saleslady. She shows Harriet and Tracy a series of stockings. The kind that stretch out into shape. She stretches stocking after stocking out on her arm. The patterns reveal themselves. Harriet likes some of the patterns and dislikes others. With a stocking stretched out on her arm, the saleslady says: 'This particular pattern reveals the meaning of life and death.' Harriet carefully examines the pattern. She watches the woman tie a knot in the top of the stocking. Harriet says: 'Yes, yes, I know. I know that it reveals the meaning of life and death. But does there have to be so much blood every single day?'

Harriet moves on to the hat department. The same saleslady shows her a hat that looks like a helmet. 'This is the latest Givenchy style, my dear. I wear one all the time now. I'll just slip it on so you can see what it looks like.' Harriet stares at her. The hat covers her eyes and ears and mouth. She wonders if it's really possible to breathe or move about without ever seeing anything. The saleslady continues chatting away as if everything is quite normal. As if she always wears a hat like that without any discomfort. Harriet considers buying the hat. If other people can live and breathe in a hat like that, why shouldn't I be able to? Maybe life would be easier in a hat like that. Maybe I wouldn't be so scared if I owned a hat like that.

Waking. Still in the stuffed chair. Staring at the figure holding a bouquet of flowers in its hand.

"I didn't think it would happen this time with you, Harriet. That's what makes me hate myself so much now. I hate myself so much I can't believe that you could still be loving me. I guess I can only go so far in a human relationship and that's all. As soon as I get involved with loving someone I start to destroy things. Then I begin to hate myself, and the more I do that, the worse I get. I don't know how to stop it, Harriet. But it's not your fault. I swear it. It's not your fault or anything to do with you. I've begun to think there's a devil in me. I don't want to treat you so badly. But I can't seem to help myself. There must be a devil in me. I hope Jimmy doesn't have one in him. I think it's from my father. Last week I actually thought of going to a priest to have it exorcized."

Moving in and out, in and around her.

"It's good to be inside you," Robert said. "I love filling your big, wet cunt."

He's treating me like an animal, Harriet thought. What is it he said before? That he'd see to me. 'Do you want to be seen to?' She wriggled beneath him.

"I'd like to swallow you," she said. "When I come, I'd like to swallow you up."

"See, baby," he said. "See how easy it is for me to relax you."

• • •

Dreaming: Of asking her brother: 'When did you first make it?' 'What do you mean, make it?' he asks. 'I mean, when did you first fuck?' 'When I was around thirty. Of course I'd fooled around before that.' 'Do you know what you are?' she asks. 'Yes, I know what I am. I'm a mama's boy and I like it. I like the noise that goes with it. And I like the battling and the coming out on top sometimes.' 'You mean,' she says, 'that you like the constant seesaw. First one person on top and then the other.' 'Yes, that's right. But you. You never could get with that. I can remember how you would lie in bed waiting to hear Ben's key in the door.' 'That's right,' she screams. 'I couldn't stand it and I never will be able to. I can't play that game.'

She stands on the ledge of a high wall. She looks down at a small, thin, and helpless-looking Robert. He calls up to her: 'Come down where I am Harriet. Hurry up and jump down here quickly or you'll miss all the fun. The bus can't wait much longer to take us to where all the fun is.' I'll end up shattered into a thousand pieces if I jump from this height. I'll be like Humpty Dumpty. They'll never be able to put me together again. Robert shouts: 'Hurry up. I can't wait all day for you. Hurry up and jump.' He must want to kill me. If he expects me to jump from this height then he must really want to kill me. How did I get up on this ledge anyway? What am I doing up here alone on this ledge? I know this much. That from up here I can watch Robert. Watch and see what he'll do next. And he can't harm me from down there. But I want to be down there in the world. I want to be down there and have some fun. I must find my own path down in my own good time, even if it means missing all the fun. She screams down to Robert: 'Go away. I won't jump. I don't want to jump and shatter into a thousand pieces. I won't. Do you hear me, Robert? I'm not your mother. I'm not my mother. I'm not your mistress. I'm not your possession. I'm not your father and I'm not Ben. I'm not coming down. I'm not you, Robert. I'd rather die up here than make that jump. Go away. Go have your fun without me.'

"I can't stand it any more, Tracy. Get Doctor Parker for me. He'll have to do something to lessen the pain. I'm too exhausted to go on. Please call him. Tell him he'll have to give me something."

Sally and Tracy converse with their eyes. Sally drops my hand. "I'll go get him," she says. "Tracy will stay here with you."

I'm alone. Separate from every other person. Sally is getting the doctor. Tracy is holding my hand. But I'm alone here. Struggling to give birth. To a premature baby.

'You're a spoiled brat. You never finish anything you start. Everything you touch turns to poison. You'll end up alone in some gutter. You're not like other respectable girls. You'll end up with nothing.'

Jeannie meeting my husband-to-be, Harvey. 'I want you to understand that this is a respectable family you're marrying into and has been for a long time. We're conventional and proud of it. We don't break the laws and we don't act like animals and we believe in doing what's right so I'm going to show you something now.'

Watching Jeannie walk towards the chest of drawers. Wondering what certified heirloom she's going to get to prove the respectability of our family.

Harvey reading the torn, crumpled-with-age piece of paper: 'This is to certify that Harriet Battenberg lost her virginity on June 15, 1940, at the age of seven, in an accident, in which, because of a fall, her hymen was broken. Signed: Louis R. Ryman: Pediatrician.'

Panicked about all the noise Jeannie made when I fell on that grate. Pain where I pee from. A doctor examining me where you're not supposed to talk about.

"It's been a long and hard labor for you, Harriet," Doctor Parker says. "Fourteen hours now. And you've been very tense and exhausted. We didn't know how tense you were when you first came here. The drug will slow the baby's trip down and make the labor still longer. But if you can't tolerate the pain, we'll give you an injection now."

"Please. Give me something right away. I can't take any more. Please."

"All right," Doctor Parker says. "Doctor Sachs. Will you prepare an injection?"

Doctor Sachs. He's the man. He's going to stop all this for me. Nice Doctor Sachs. Yes. Yes. There's my arm. Take it. Take it and stop the feeling.

Searching for the bottle of liquid that will stop the feeling. Locking the bathroom door. Like I do when I come in here to masturbate. That won't help now. Nothing will. So examine the inside of the medicine chest. For the bottle that will end this life. The iodine bottle. That's the one. With the black skull and bones. *Please keep this bottle out of the reach of children.* I'm not a child. I'm fourteen. And I can reach it. Swallow it down. I can't swallow what she keeps saying about me and Martin. And Ben's beating. Why Ben? So swallow the iodine. In one gulp. I wonder if it's painful. Too painful a way to die. Too slow and torturous. Will she care if I really do die? No. It will give her a chance to tell everybody that there always was something wrong with her Harriet. I can hear her saying: 'I knew it for a long time. There was something different about her. She wasn't like other girls of her age. Her father made her that way. By being too nice to her.' If I kill myself it will prove that she was right about me. She won't even cry. Won't even feel badly. Just be able to tell Ben: 'I told you so. You've made a mess of her.'

And Ben. How will he feel? If I kill myself. If I finish off the job he started when he beat me as if he wanted to kill me. If I'm really dead will he understand how unjust he was with me? Feel sorry for doing it? He used to protect me from her. Reassure me that I wasn't the piece of trash she treats me like. Where has my brother Harvey been all these months? He's stayed away from this massacre. He used to protect me from her. Now everyone in this house thinks I'm a disgusting, dirty, filthy-minded slut. Now they all know about me. God, Ben. What did I do to make you want to kill me? Something. Or you wouldn't have hit me. Not you, Ben. I'll kill myself. Then you'll understand, Ben. How horribly you treated me. And I'll be too dead to listen to any more of her words or feel any more of your cruelty.

Banging on the bathroom door. 'Hey, Harriet. Get out of there.' Harvey's voice shouting: 'I've been waiting to get into the bathroom for half an hour. Get the hell out of there already.'

Useless iodine bottle. Put back in its place on the shelf. Next to the bottle of Milk of Magnesia. Exercise completed. Not even my death would get them to understand how they've mistreated me. But it would end living here in this hateful house. Life is hopeless in this apartment. So I'll make myself scarce. Stay out of it as much as I can. In a few years I can get away from here. To the University. Work on that. Do everything I can to get away. To a school fifty billion miles away from here. But in the meantime. Play dead. Just for a little while. Until I can get out of this hell. I'll play dead like Skippy does when Ben says: 'Roll over on your back, Skippy, and play dead.' And Skippy rolls over and lies dead still. Until Ben says: 'O.K. Good dog. O.K., Skippy. Now live.' And Skippy jumps up. Alive and waiting for his doggy biscuit. O.K., Harriet. Play dead. In a few years from now I can jump up and live. When I'm far away from here.

Planting the seeds for all those dreams later. Of the poor little baby locked in the cage. Has no body. Only a head. Well live in it then. Keep my thoughts away from them and live in my head. Lock them out. Lock myself in.

Hours alone. Baby-sitting for Mrs. Fine. Imagining. Meeting Martin one day. I'll have two children. A little boy holding one of my hands. A little girl in the other. I'll be taking them to Manhattan to see a puppet show. They'll look beautiful. So will I. In a big brimmed hat I'll look beautiful. I'll meet Martin in the subway train. By accident. I'll be married and it will be safe to talk with him. We'll meet by mistake and I'll explain to him. How I had to stop seeing him and not go to any more camp parties because of what they did to me. He'll understand that it wasn't me who wanted to stop seeing him. Just because he's black. It was them. And when the children and I get home that night I'll tell the children's father. I'll tell my nice husband how I ran into Martin. I'll tell him how we talked. And he'll understand and love me. Very much.

"Do you feel better now, Harriet?" Doctor Parker asks. "Is the drug working for you yet?"

"Yes. Thank you for giving it to me. I feel better."

They've started-two-three-four and out-two-three-for how long will it last-two-three-four an-hour-three-four-five-a second-two-three-four there's-the top of the mountain now come down slowly-four-five-six-only to start up again-two-three-after the climax the pain lets up-seven-eight-nine-to start again so breathe to the rhythm of the pain-three-four-because you can't change the rhythm only stay with it-four-five-six-until the end and linger with the ending-three-four-five-the pleasure in that last pulsation of pain-six-seven-eight-the relief-nine-ten-eleven. Don't linger with it for too long. Start resting. There isn't much time before the pain attacks again. Sleep. Rest. Before it all starts again. There are a million more centuries to get through. I've been in labor all my life but the baby in me isn't born yet. Stop thinking. Rest.

"The drug is working. The pain wasn't so bad this time."

"Good," Doctor Parker says.

It's working for me. It will have to work for me. Until I can get out of this house. Imagine. Imagine what it will be like when the Prince—The Prince who understands and protects and knows everything—comes along. Imagine the years before that. A billion miles away from here at a big university where no one will know the street I lived on before. The things—the terrible things they said I did before. What they said about how contaminated I am. Imagine breathing in air that they have not exhaled into. Where I'll be able to be myself. The self I'm hiding from everybody now because they'll get me if I show it. How sweet. How very sweet I'll smile at Martin when I explain it all to him. But in the mean time. Stay out of their way and don't do anything they can get me for.

'No, John. But thanks. I don't like basketball games or sororities or parties or high school boys with acne.'

'No thank you, Peter. I'm going to the movies with my girl friend Elise tonight. And I'm staying at her house for the week end. High school girls who can't think of anything but making up and dates with their boy friends make me sick.'

'No, Phillip. I'm not imprisoned at home. I can go out if I want to.'

'I know, Frank, that they voted me one of the prettiest girls in the class. That doesn't mean that I can't stay at home on Saturday night and read, thank you.'

I like baby-sitting every week end. Mr. and Mrs. Fine are so nice to each other and they know how to have fun together and I can tell that they like each other. They go out every Saturday. Like I will with my Prince. And I'll be such a good mother. I'll love my children and they'll be beautiful and he and I will be like Mr. and Mrs. Fine who love each other and not like Ben and Jeannie. And my little boy will be like her little boy. Pretty and always laughing.

It's safe baby-sitting. They can't say anything against my baby-sitting. Besides I make fifty cents an hour. 'I know I don't need the money, Elise. But I like taking care of that little boy. You know I don't like parties any more.'

Later when I get out of here I'll live. Dead for now. I know I'm not really dead. 'No, Elise. You're wrong. They haven't put me in prison for what I did. I don't want to go out. Not now.'

But I must take the Ben who beat me into the escape plans. He's got to say yes. I want to go to the University and study sociology. Learn to be a social worker. To help other people. I don't want to go to a university that's close to this house. I want to go far far away. Michigan University. That's a thousand miles from here. And I have to get Ben to agree and pay.

Jeannie screaming: 'I say she should go to New York University. She should live at home. A girl like her needs watching. But if you're mad enough to pay for her away from home then don't come to me when she ends up in the gutter.'

Let her rant. Let her rave. Just keep on baby-sitting and working on Ben so that he agrees. And go to summer school so I can get out of high school early. But I've got to get away soon or I'll die.

Chasing me through my night life. Hungry lions and tigers. Play dead. Don't move. Freeze like a statue. That way they won't get me.

Being tossed, turned, and twisted in the mile-high and mile-long washing machine. Sensation of swinging like when I was very little and pushed up so high that it felt all funny coming down. But in this dream it hurts. Really hurts. Finally the man comes. Takes me out of the machine. 'Am I clean now? Tell me. Am I clean enough now?' 'Cleaner than when we put you into the machine, young lady. But you are definitely not contamination free. So give us your high school diploma. We'll stamp it STILL CONTAMINATED. That means that you can be set free now. But you cannot enter areas where there are large groups of people whom you can contaminate.' Getting hysterical. 'But I want to go to the University. I must go to the University. And there are a lot of people in each class.' 'I'm sorry, young lady. I've stamped your diploma: STILL CONTAMINATED.'

That's only a dream. Forget about what Ben did and get him to talk Jeannie into letting me go away. Far away.

No matter how far away I go the contractions find me. Find me and start their own cycle. There's nothing I can do to stop them or make them slower or faster or more gentle. They are more powerful than me. All I can do to keep from screaming is to follow them. Vibration by vibration with in-two-three-four and out-two-three-four. There is only now and no future for me to live in-two-three-four-until the last one starts to go down and downer until-two-three-four-it isn't there any more and to make sure I just keep breathing out-five-six-seven-eight-nine-and collapse. Into a heap of weary nothingness.

Tracy's hand loosens in mine. Sally drops my other hand. They're collapsing with me so they can be back with me when it starts all over again. For how many years have they been holding my hands and going through this with me and where's Robert's hand?

Robert wanted to kill me. And the baby in me. But Robert told me how easy it was to love me. Told me he cared about me. What happened to Robert? What happened to Ben? I did something. Something terrible. That's why Robert's hand isn't here.

'You'll see, you brat. One day you'll see. What men are like. Only women can understand the suffering of other women. When the going gets rough the men say good-bye. Go out and have a good time. I'm the only one who cares about you. Not your father.'

Ten years old. Wishing Jeannie would die and let me alone. Stop picking on me. Writing on the wall next to my bed with my finger nail: I wish my mother was dead. Horrified by thinking that combination of words. Rubbing hard with the palm of my hand. Erasing those invisible words. Before anyone sees or hears them.

Sally and Tracy sit up in attention. They sense the contractions are about to start again. They take my hands as I begin to pant-two-three-four.

December 15. Watching Robert flinging his arms and shouting.

Harriet stood paralyzed. She stared at herself staring with disbelief at Robert.

"What do you mean, Harriet? What do you mean what am I going to do? I'll tell you what I'm going to do. I'm going to burn down this flat. Kill you. Never give you or that baby any money. Never see you. Kill you. That's what I'm going to do. Do you hear me? That's what I'm going to do."

"Yes, Robert. I hear you. Now for God's sake get yourself out of here. Leave me alone."

"Don't tell me to get out of my own flat. This flat is mine. Stop pushing me out. Stop trying to get rid of me. I'm going."

He slammed the door. She rushed downstairs to the kitchen and started to wash the dishes.

Don't panic, Harriet. Don't panic. Just lock the door. What if he comes back and finds the door locked? He'll really flip. Don't panic. He can't really kill you. Understand what he means. He's just doing everything to rid himself of all thoughts of you. He can't cope with his own behavior. He doesn't mean he's going to really kill you. He just wants to erase you from his thoughts. Like when you dreamed of killing him. He's not going to burn down this flat and you don't need his money. Keep calm. It's just his way of telling you that he's incapable of getting out of the hell he feels. He wants you dead. Out of his life. Stop shaking. He's not going to kill you. Not really. He won't come back in a few moments with a knife. Stop worrying about what to expect from him next. There's nothing to worry about. He wouldn't really kill you. If for no other reason than he doesn't want to spend the rest of his life in jail. He just has to imagine an existence without you. He wants you dead for him. That's all. Don't panic. Think about all those things he told you last night. How it isn't your fault. How there's a devil in him. How he feels so small that he thinks he's going to disappear. How he hates himself so much that he can't understand how you could still like him. Remember what he said. 'It's the living together in this flat, Harriet.' That's what he said. 'I didn't think this would happen again. It's happened every time I've lived with a woman. Not that I'm screwing around all over town like I did when Anna was pregnant. Just that I have to be with people who would bore you. With good reason they'd bore you. But when I have to be with them I flip. Because I think I'll start fucking around and then I end up all depressed and hating myself.' Think about what he said. 'I can only go so far with a human relationship, Harriet, and no farther. Relationships only mean something to me up to a certain point. I can only be constructive when I'm not involved with someone I really love. I didn't think this would happen again, Harriet. All I'm able to do is to hurt you. I always hurt those good things I come into contact with. I don't want to hurt you, Harriet. It's that devil. It's not your fault. See, Harriet. It's not your fault. It's me.'

"Stop worrying. He said all those things last night. Just keep remembering them. He won't burn down this flat and he won't kill me. And he knows it's not my fault. He said so. Now make a cup of tea and then lie down for a minute. He won't come back today. After the tea, have a rest. After that I can decide what to do. Maybe even call Sue or Tony or someone. Tell them what happened. They'll tell you that Robert won't really do anything to hurt you. Someone objective will know that. Anyone who knows Robert will know that. But double lock the door. No, don't do that. That might really flip him. If he tries to get into his flat and can't. Tea. Make tea. And stop shaking. It's no good for the baby. All this. Even if I give it up after it's born. Besides I'm not going to give it away for adoption. I know that. I was only testing Robert when I suggested I might. I just wanted desperately to hear him say: 'Don't be foolish, darling. You know I love you and want the baby and want you.' But he didn't. Just said: 'Well if you are going to give it away, why don't you at least think about giving it to someone we know.' Now. Don't hurt it. It's helpless. That's what it is. I'm treating it as badly in my womb as Jeannie treated me. Stop killing the baby. It's Robert I want to kill. Not the baby. He's abandoning me at the time I most need him. Don't do the same to the baby. Don't be Jeannie or Ben. Hang on to the little bit of you that's left. Try, Harriet. Or you'll crack up. Quietly. Not like Robert. I'll crack up alone in this room with the echo of my own thoughts, and louder still the echo of Robert's words. 'I'm going to kill you, Harriet. That's what I'm going to do.' Drink your tea and shut up. Rest. There's nothing he can do to me any more or any worse than he's already done.

December 16.   Ringing telephone.

Harriet jumped up to stop the sound.

"This is New York City calling. For Harriet Stein."

"Yes, speaking."

"Just one moment please. Go ahead New York."

"Hello, Harriet. It's me, Tracy."

"Tracy? Hello. How are you?"

"Great. And how are you and your big belly? Beautiful I bet."

"I'm all right, Tracy. How's the show going?"

"It's a big success. Everything from London is these days. They've made a big star out of me. But never mind all that. It's you I'm interested in. You, that baby in you and Robert. Wish I could be there to see you all swinging. How is Robert?"

"Robert. He's O.K. Lots of television work at the moment."

"What's the matter, Harriet? You're not so happy to hear from me that you're crying, are you? What's the matter?"

"It's good to hear your voice, Tracy. That's all. I've missed you and it's good to hear your voice."

"I know that, baby. That's why I called you. I've been thinking a lot about you and that belly. Harriet, come on. Tell me. What's up? Why are you crying?"

'Because, Tracy. Because it's all gone wrong. Robert's pulled a Doctor Jekyll and Mr. Hyde on me."

"What do you mean, Harriet? What's happening?"

"I don't know. All I do know is that Robert's flipped out and I'm going with him. He's become more and more sadistic and bullying every day. I can't understand any of what's happened. All I know is that I'm a nervous wreck. Every time Robert comes home I feel I better get out. And when he's here the tension is like there's a time bomb ticking away. The telephone bell a few minutes ago had me jumping to the ceiling. I'm frightened, Tracy. For the baby. And for myself."

"Listen, Harriet. Stop crying and listen to me. I don't exactly understand what's happening, but it sounds a bit like the Robert-of-Anna days. So why don't you get away from him for a bit. What month are you in now?"

"The very end of the sixth."

"I've an idea. Why don't you fly over for a few weeks? Spend Christmas with me. I've an enormous flat here in New York. Sally and Bill are living upstairs. We could all hang out together over the holidays. Sing Christmas carols and all that rot."

"I'm not much in the mood for celebrations, Tracy. I'm a wreck."

"You sound it. If Robert can't give you what you need now, we all can. Lots of love and don't forget, baby, I'm in the land of the delicatessens. Two of them just around the corner. But joking aside. Why don't you come? I'll have everything taken care of from this end. Ticket and stuff like that so you don't have to think about anything. You can pay me later."

"I don't know, Tracy. I don't know about it. But I have thought about getting away from Robert for a bit. I thought I'd go to Ibiza or somewhere close."

"Don't be silly. You'll be here in no time by plane. Any why go somewhere like Ibiza. The doctors stink there. And in case you have to see one you can get great care here in N.Y.C."

"I don't think so. I don't think New York is such a good idea now. And I've got those natural childbirth classes starting in three weeks."

"You'll be back in three weeks. Come as soon as you're ready. Like Saturday. I'll get a three-week excursion ticket for you. So what if you miss a few classes? You can catch up when you get back."

"It sounds appealing, Tracy."

"Then don't think about it. Just get ready and come. You sound needy and we'll feed you."

"Thanks. It's all very good. Your voice. Your offer.

Let me think about it. And I've got to check with the doctor. To see if it's safe for me to fly. But I don't know about New York."

"If you're worried about your parents, forget it. You don't have to let them know you're here. Now get on the phone to your doctor and call me back tonight. I'll be home. I don't go to the theater tonight. Do you hear me? Get yourself over here. I want you to come."

"O.K., Tracy. Thanks for calling. I'll call you back tonight. Or tomorrow morning."

"O.K. Now listen. I love you and so do Sally and Bill. You ought to be around some love now. Probably be good for Robert too. Give him a chance to think about what he's been up to. Don't forget the time difference between London and New York when you call me back."

"No. I won't. Thanks again, Tracy. I'll speak with you later. Bye."

"Good-bye. And cool it. Everything is going to be all right."

"Bye."

Sitting on the bed.

Now rest. Sit down and rest and think about Tracy's call. Maybe you should go to New York. No need to worry about Ben and Jeannie. You don't have to call them. It would be nice though to see Ben. He'd be nice to me now. He'd understand. I wouldn't have to tell him about this hellish scene. Just that I felt like coming to New York before I had the baby. That I'm not married but that I'm going to get married when the baby is born. And Jeannie. She'd be nice to me now. When she sees that I'm pregnant. She'll be nice. Besides, if I don't want to I don't have to call them. Like Tracy said. But it would be nice to see Ben.

Drinking tea. On the couch.

"Robert, I'd like to talk to you for a moment," Harriet said. "I spoke with Tracy on the phone today."

"Oh. Did you call her?"

"No. She called me. This morning."

"How is she? How's the show going?"

"She's fine. The show's a big success."

"Good. I suppose you want to talk to me about staying away from this flat again. Well, I bloody well have to pop in and out for some of my things. Is that it? Is that what you want to talk to me about? Well go ahead. If you can talk above the piano playing going on in the flat upstairs."

"No. That's not exactly what I wanted to talk to you about."

"One of these days," Robert shouted, "I'm going to

throw a petrol bomb into those bastards' window up there. That'll stop that rotten music. And as for my staying at the studio. I can't. Until Tony gives me back that bedding he took from me six months ago. One of these days I'll blow up his car and let the air out of his tires. I've asked him five times for that bedding."

"Robert. I'm thinking of going to New York. For a few weeks."

"What? Now? At Christmas time? I suppose Tracy told you that you better get away from that disgusting creature you're living with. I suppose that's it, isn't it?"

"No. That's not it. It's that I can't get any peace around here. If it's not me you're threatening to kill, it's Tony or the neighbors. You can see the effect on me."

"What do you mean? Kill you? I never said anything like that. And if I did, I didn't mean it. But if you think I did. Well then go. Go to New York and have a ball there over Christmas."

"I'm not going to have a ball, Robert. I'm going to get away from this scene for a while."

"No reason why you shouldn't have a ball anyway. Except of course you'll be too embarrassed and self-conscious to fuck anyone with that fat belly of yours."

"That's the limit, Robert. You really are disgusting. But that's it. You can't get me to go crawling around on the floor any more than you've already done. I was stupid enough, just stupid enough to hope that you'd do something to keep me from going. Anything. Like saying, 'Is it safe for you to travel now?' Anything. But I can't kid myself any more. You don't give a shit if I live or die. Or if your baby lives or dies. Now do me a favor and stay away from here for just a few days. Long enough for me to get out of here. And I'll do you a favor and get out of your way. I'm not thinking any more about going to New York. I'm going."

"It looks like you're almost there now," Doctor Parker says. "You're going into the final stage. Just before your baby will be born."

"I'm almost there?"

"Yes, Harriet. It won't be long now. A half hour or so before you'll be ready to give birth. I'll be back shortly."

I'm almost there. I'll wash my face and comb my hair. The train is almost in New York City now. I'm almost home. Don't forget. I'm fourteen now. It's about time Harvey started treating me like a woman instead of a little kid. I've changed this summer at camp. I've changed a lot and I bleed now. I wonder if I'd rather be a man and shave every day or a woman and bleed once a month? Well I'm a woman and that's that. But I won't be like other women. I'll work like men do. No beauty salons and tea parties for me. What counts is that I'm not a kid any more. I'm a woman now. About time Harvey started treating me like one. I've got to get Harvey to notice that I've changed. So that he treats me differently. Like a young lady. I'll wear sweaters. Not too tight. But tight enough for Harvey to see that I've got breasts. No lipstick yet but my hair looks different. This style makes me look older. And I'll act differently. Sweet and ladylike. I won't let him boss me around any more. He's got to stop treating me like a kid and calling me fatty. Oh, Harvey. How different I'll be. You'll want to introduce me to your boy friends instead of telling me to beat it. And I'm very smart now. You'll want to talk to me about world affairs. I'm interested in them. You'll see. And of course I won't suck my thumb so you won't have anything to scream at me at night for when you're trying to sleep. And I can stay up late now and lie in bed and read. Just like you do. I'll be a little lady so you'll have to treat me like one. You'll want to.

'Hello, fatty. Good to see you home from camp. But get out of the room for a while. Make yourself scarce. I've got exams coming up next week. Hey, that's quite a scarf you're wearing around your neck. Give it to me. I want to wear it.'

"Tracy, listen. The injection is wearing off. I want another one. Right away. Tell the doctor that I want another shot of something."

"O.K., Harriet. I'll go get him. But don't forget what he said. It won't be long now. They're getting the operating room ready for you."

It won't be long now. The plane is about to land at La Guardia Airport. 'Fasten your seat belts please.' I'm almost home. I've been away at the University for over a year. A thousand miles away from home. Like I wanted to be. I'll tell Jeannie all about it. About how much I've learned. What a wonderfully exciting year I've had. What good grades I got and about all the new people I met. Don't forget. Jeannie never had the chance to go to a university even though she got out of high school with such good grades. Her father wouldn't let her go. Sent her to work in a factory. So try. Try and make her understand how thankful I am that she let me go. And tell her all about it so she can be happy for me. So she's treated me badly. Forget it. Try hard to talk to her. Make her understand what a thrill it's been to have such marvellous teachers and how beautiful university life is. How stimulated and alive it's made me feel. Make her understand. She'll understand.

'And you're not going back to that university come hell or high water. I know all about your free love activities there and all about the communist organizations you belong to. You bet I know. I have proof. That whore of a girl friend of yours, Sheila Booth. I know all about her too. Her mother called me up when she got back from visiting that hot bed for communist activities and sexual orgies. I know that the organizations you and that tramp belong to are all on McCarthy's list. Black-lists. You'll all end up in prison where you belong. Locked up. Not on my dead body are you going back to that school. You can just start getting that idea out of your head. And if you want to go to a university any more you'll go to a city college and live here at home like other decent girls do. Where I can watch you. You need someone to control you or you just run haywire. If I had my way you'd be going to a school and learning to type so you could get a good job instead of learning all those highfalutin things that only lead to sex and communism. But that father of yours. He had to be smart and let you go to a university. Well, now he can see what you've learned there.'

"Tracy. How long will it be? I don't think I can

stand another contraction. Not one more bit of pain. God, Tracy. Squeeze my hand. They're starting all over again."

"Not long, love. Not long. Doctor Parker says so."

It won't be long now. I'm almost home. So close that I can see the Statue of Liberty. It's been a great boat trip. I'm all excited. First time back in the United States after three years in Europe. Ben will be thrilled. I've been all over Europe. At last I've seen all those places he's always talked so much about to me. All those places he saw as a soldier in the First World War. That must have been exciting for him. The kid from Forest Hills, New York, getting away from home and mum for the first time. And the last. If it hadn't been for that war he never would have left Forest Hills. What a ball it will be to talk to him about Scotland. Home of his much talked about mistress. Cruel of him though to talk about her all the time in front of Jeannie. And to slip her photograph into Jeannie's family picture album. Anyway. We'll talk of his gay Paree and foggy London. I'll be back in London in six weeks. He'll get a kick out of that too. Me writing for a top fashion magazine in London. Living there and working at an important job. Well, he'll think it's important anyway. Even if I'm sick of writing that trash. But while I'm here in New York I'll have a great time. Ben and I will really talk. I'll hear all his stories over again but with a different ear. I'm ready now to see Ben as another person. Not just as my father. It will be double kicks this time. I've seen that little town in Scotland. Too bad I couldn't find his mistress. Now I understand why Ben had to come back after the war. His mother would have flipped if he'd married someone who wasn't Jewish. And Ben's attached to his mother. We'll talk of Europe, and the fun of it all. Of course, I won't mention all those lonely, scared moments I had. Feeling the stranger so much of the time and displaced—misplaced. But we'll laugh and talk of the gaiety of it all.

'Listen, kid. It sounds like you've been having a great time. Running around the world. I know what it's like. I did it myself when I was a young man. But don't you think it's time you settled down? Found some decent guy and settled down. Have a few kids with a guy who can give you security. Start living in the good old United States of America again. It's not so bad here you know. You've sown your wild oats. Like I did, kid. But don't you think it's time you settled down? You sure are your old man's daughter, kid. A real run-around. You like a good time just like your father. But don't take it too far, kid. You're not getting any younger you know. Find yourself a husband. Not like that first guy you had. And settle down. You can cheat a bit after that if you have to. You know what I mean. Don't you, kid?'

"It's all right, Harriet," Tracy says. "Doctor Parker will be here in a minute."

'In ten minutes our plane will be landing at Kennedy Airport. Please refrain from smoking and fasten your seat belts.'

'Get me a bag. Quickly please. I'm sick. Very sick.'

'Come this way, madame. You'll be better off at the front of the plane. Come this way quickly. You've had a rough flight, madame. But we're almost there now. There. You'll feel better now. With this wet cloth on your head. Is that a bit better?'

'Yes, a bit. Thank you. But I'm sick. Very sick.'

'I know how it is for you. Must be a terrible feeling. What with you being so far gone. When is your baby due?'

'In a few months. But I'm sick now. Help me.'

'It will be all right now. We've landed. You just sit there, madame. You're pale as a ghost. We're arranging to get you a wheel chair to take you quickly through Customs. You're in no condition to walk. You look like a ghost. Do you feel a bit better?'

'Yes, a little.'

'Honestly, Mary. You'd think women would know better than to travel on an airplane when they're almost about to pop. Oh well. It takes all kinds.'

Wheeling through Customs. Maybe I will tell Ben. I want to tell Ben. How awful the scene has been these last few months. How sick I've been with it all. Tell him the truth about why I came to New York. How I had to get away. What a loveless maniac Robert turned into. Maybe he'll understand. Feel sorry for me. No, I won't tell him. Maybe I won't even call him from Tracy's. Maybe I won't even let him know I'm in New York. There's no sense in worrying him. Besides, there's nothing he can do for me anyway. And he'd rather not hear any of my troubles. But maybe he'd want to know. Maybe he'd understand if I told him. I want to see him. I need to see him. Think about it later. You're here. In New York City. What about Jeannie? Surely she'll be different. She knows what it's like to be pregnant. At least that's one thing we'll have in common. Maybe she'll behave like a mother now. A sympathetic mother. There's Tracy. Go on and wave. Smile. Like everything is O.K.

Tracy greeting me: 'Now tell me all about it. What happened between you and Robert. I'm so glad you came. Everything's going to be great now you're here in New York. Who knows? You might even decide to stay longer. In a few weeks I'll be out of the show and with nothing to do. We can play together then. I'm so glad you've come.'

Doctor Parker's voice: "Everything is O.K. You've been marvelous. And it's almost over. Now tell me, Harriet. Do you think you can remain conscious for the birth? You've gone through these fourteen hours splendidly. And you've done the natural childbirth exercises beautifully. So I understand how important it's been for you to be aware of what's been happening. Now tell me. Do you have the strength to go on until the baby is born? I think you're more exhausted than any of us here realized until now. But I know how much you want to be awake for the birth."

Don't answer. Don't answer whoever it is asking those questions. Not-two-three-four-until they're over-four-five-six-seven-eight-nine. There. It's Doctor Parker. He wants to know something. About whether I can go through with the birth without more drugs. Well, I can't. I just can't. Oh my God. They're starting again. Only a split second now to rest before they start again. Concentrate-two-three-four.

'Listen, mister. You can't go on driving so fast. You see mister, I'm pregnant. Very pregnant. In my seventh month. And I'm getting dizzy from the speed of this taxicab. And nauseous.'

'You women. I don't understand you. What the hell are you doing out on Christmas Eve in a cab, lady? If you're so far gone. Think you're superwoman or something. And if you're suffering why didn't you tell me sooner? I've been speeding, lady, because I want to get home. No cab driver wants to work on Christmas Eve. I got a couple of kids myself. And the old bag. She lost two before she had our Johnny. Why didn't you tell me sooner that you're pregnant. I don't have eyes in the back of my head. But anyway. You shouldn't be out in all this traffic on Christmas Eve. Hey. Where's your old man anyway?'

'He's in London. That's where he is.'

'Well I know it's none of my business, lady. But you shouldn't be gallivanting about alone in your condition on a Christmas Eve. Not in all this traffic. Could make me sick. No less someone in your condition, lady.'

You're almost there, so stop worrying. He's right. You shouldn't have come out tonight. But I couldn't stand another minute of listening to Tracy tell me that all this wouldn't have happened if I'd married Robert and acted more dependent on him and made him feel more like a man. And you should have told the driver to slow down a long time ago. He's right about that too. You're almost there though. Tracy's apartment is just up the street. Thank goodness for that.

'Tracy, I feel ill. Very ill.'

'Well, sit down. I'll make you a cup of tea. You really are stupid. Why the hell did you go out? Don't you remember what a nightmare of traffic and noise New York is on Christmas Eve? Why the hell do you treat yourself so badly? You could have stayed here and I would have cooked dinner or something. You're stupid to have gone out. Especially as you've been feeling so ill since you got to New York.'

'I don't know Tracy. I don't know why I went out. But there are blood stains on my panties.'

'Blood stains. Why didn't you tell me the minute you got in?'

'Because I just went to the bathroom.'

'Are you sure? Sure they're blood stains? This isn't a false alarm or something? Is it?'

'Yes. I'm sure. You better call a doctor. Right away.'

'I will. Right away. I'll call my analyst. He'll recommend someone good. I know he will.'

"How do you feel," Doctor Parker asks.

"Sick. Sick with exhaustion. Please give me another shot. Of anything. I can't go on. Not another minute."

"If we put you out now you won't be able to help us through the birth. And you won't be conscious for it. Seems a pity after all you've been through. But you know best."

Yes. I know best. I know I can't take any more. Not any more.

'You're a spoiled brat, that's what you are. Never finish anything you start. But you're out of my hands. Your father has made you into what you are and there's nothing I can do about it. God knows I've tried to be a good mother.'

'You're still the kid who's got to be different, aren't

you kid? Why the hell didn't you get married if the guy wanted to marry you. Who is the guy anyway?'

Who is Robert and where is Ben and if you could see me now, Robert—can you see me now?—how would you feel about yourself and would you see how cruel you've been and would you leave me alone and stop trying to kill me and my baby? And I thought it was going to be different, so different that you would help me have this baby and not want me to disappear and I am disappearing.

"Yes, Doctor Parker, I want to be put out. Put me out. Please. Get me out of all this."

December 20. Dining in Tracy's New York kitchen.

"Before Tracy gets home," Jeannie said, "we better have a talk. We're your family, Harriet, and we're the ones who really care about you now. You should come home to Forest Hills and stay there with us. Things can't be any good in England if you come to New York when you're pregnant. You don't have to explain. Just come home and I'll take care of you. Stay here in America near your family. You've had enough of living

151

in a strange country. I'll take care of you until the baby's born if you come and live with us. Women like us have to be very careful. Miscarriages and trouble with births run in our family. You know how many miscarriages I had before I finally had you. We know what's best for you. Maybe we haven't been the best parents, but we can live and learn, can't we? You come home to live and I'll take care of you and your baby."

"Thanks, mother. But like I said. I'm only here on a three-week excursion trip. I'm living with a man in London. And while I'm here I'm staying with Tracy. I want to be in the city."

"A fine specimen of a man he must be. Letting you make a trip like this when you're so pregnant. Your family means nothing to you. Never has and never will. You just use us for what you can get out of us. You're rotten."

"Listen, Jeannie. I'll see you often while I'm here. I'll come out to Forest Hills. But you must understand that my home and my life are in London now."

"If you can't come home to live I don't want you coming out to Forest Hills at all. I don't want anyone in the neighborhood to see you in your condition and not married. I'm too old and sick to deal with what the neighbors will say. If you can't do the decent thing and come home and stay here in America and let me help you and your baby then you can just go back to that country you call your home. Go back to your friends, as you call them. And let that actress, Tracy, take care of you here in New York. She and the likes of her are just like you. Without morals. Like poison to an upstanding society. Go. Go back to England and don't come visiting me. I wish you'd never called. I'm too sick to stand all this. I'm going to get my coat. It's time we went. Don't you think so, Ben?"

"Yes," Ben said. "I guess it is late."

He looked at Harriet. "You're still a weirdy, aren't you, kid? Still got to be different. If you think you're going to get married, and believe you me you ought to, why didn't you just lie? You should have told your mother that you're already married. She's gone all crazy now. And I'll have to listen to her rave about it. All day and night. She'll never stop."

"Harriet. Harriet. Wake up now, Harriet. It's over now, Harriet."

Whispered words accompanied by gentle rubbing of the shoulder.

I open my eyes. A man there telling me to wake up Harriet.

"Wake up now. It's over now, Harriet."

I must be Harriet. He's telling me to wake up now. There's a man standing over me. Smiling. I'll smile back. Smiling muscles. I'm in heaven. I'm an angel or a child. Or an imbecile. Whoever I am I'm smiling back at the man in the white jacket. White jacket. Man. Doctor. Hospital. He has a nice smile on his mouth. In his eyes. Smile to the nice man.

"Hello, Harriet. It's all right now. Wake up."

Sounds entering my ears. Louder. Making words. Nice words. Keep smiling. It feels so good here.

"It's all over now, Harriet. You're fine."

I'm Harriet and I'm fine. And he's smiling. Everything must be very beautiful here.

"And you've had a baby girl."

He's telling someone that they've had a baby girl. Harriet had a baby girl. That's nice. Very very nice. Smiling at the smiling nice man.

"Harriet, can you hear me? You're fine."

Harriet is fine. Isn't that nice? He's telling me something. I'm Harriet and I've had a baby girl. He's still smiling so I'm still smiling back at him.

"Harriet. You're fine."

I'm fine. And I'm Harriet.

"But the baby is in some danger."

He's telling me something. The baby is in danger. Why am I still smiling? Because he's smiling. Somebody's baby is in danger.

"Harriet, can you hear me now? It's all over and you're fine. But your baby is in some danger."

Your baby and you're Harriet and your baby is in danger. But it's all over now. The man says so. He's the doctor. I'm the Harriet who's had a baby girl and she's in danger. But Harriet is fine.

"She's in an incubator for premature babies and we'll wheel you past her now on the way back to your room. You can look at her for a moment."

Movement. Rock-a-bye Harriet's had a baby girl.

"There. You can't see much of her because she's got a mask on. To help her breathe. You see. She's very tiny."

Poor baby. Poor baby is very tiny and she's got a little muzzle on to help her breathe.

December 25. Eight hours later. The baby girl died.

AFTERWORD

Nineteen sixty-nine was a banner year for the exploding second wave of American feminism. The disturbance and the excitement of thousands of women suddenly "speaking out" was echoed everywhere, and nowhere more loudly than in publishing. That year alone we had Alix Kates Shulman's *Memoirs of An Ex-Prom Queen*, Margaret Atwood's *The Edible Woman*, Ursula Le Guin's *The Left Hand of Darkness*, an influential history of the women's rights movement (William O'Neill's *Everyone Was Brave*), and on the front

158

page of the *New York Times Book Review*, Lila Karp's *The Queen Is in the Garbage*.

Today, these books are read as stirring contributions to the literature of testament that grew out of an extraordinary period in American cultural history, the one characterized by the rise of the liberationist movements—blacks, gays, women—that have proven the United States's enduring contribution to twentieth-century world politics. The novels, especially—all received with wonder and interest upon publication—constitute the kind of social documentation that literature so often provides: a vivid recreation of the way it felt on the ground during a time of immense social upheaval.

The Queen Is in the Garbage, Lila Karp's strongly autobiographical novel, is emblematic of the work that seemed to be storming the country, proliferating especially among the women who had always been most taken for granted: the ultra-respectable "nice girls." Karp herself—for many years now a highly successful feminist educator and psychotherapist—was, in her thirties, typical of those who, in 1969, felt compelled to join the ranks of those speaking out.

It remains one of life's great mysteries, that moment of readiness in the life of an idea whose time has come when, a complaint blossoms into an imperative and in no time at all bursts into open demand. If you are one who responds to

159

the moment, you can never really explain it, you can only describe what it felt like.

Somewhere around 1968—that fabled year of social protest—women all over the United States seemed spontaneously to be asking, How did I get here? Why do I feel at worst off the map, at best at the margin; either way not centered; without agency; never at one with my life; as though, wherever I am, *it* is elsewhere?

First, it was women in leftwing politics who began speaking out, but almost immediately on their heels came hundreds and then thousands: women who had never used their education, women for whom romantic love had been the raison d'etre, women who had occupied the second or third rank in their profession for no reason other than that they were women. Suddenly, masses of them were old enough, bored enough, exhausted and pained enough to begin formulating the kind of answers to questions that had, every fifty years or so since the French Revolution, heralded a renewal of the women's rights movement: the one that had been variously composed of those called New Women, Odd Women, Free Women, and, in the 1970s, Liberated Women.

When 70s feminists began reading their own history, they discovered that, whatever the reincarnated label, in each generation a single realization had prevailed. It was this: The idea that men by nature take their brains seriously, and women by nature do not, is an ingrained belief that serves the culture and from it flows the entirety of all our lives. The assumption, shared by both sexes, that a female person was not naturally fitted to be a worker in the world's enterprise, was the central dilemma of a woman's existence. The insight, in every generation of feminists, had come like Revelation. And, like Revelation, it lit up a convert's sky.

One feels joy when a sufficiently large number of people are powered by a social explanation of how their lives have taken shape and are gathered together in the same place at the same time, speaking the same language, making the same analysis, meeting again and again in restaurants, lecture halls, and apartments for the pleasure of elaborating the insights and repeating the analyses. It is the joy of revolutionary politics, and in the 70s, all you had to do was open your mouth and inhale, the air was full of it. To be an American feminist in those years—bliss was it in that dawn to be alive. Not an I-love-you in the world could touch it.

At the same time, although the rhetoric ran high, sounding at times like religious fervor, 70s feminists soon came to realize that, although they stood united in political analysis, only individually could, rescue themselves. As Anton Chekhov had so memorably put it, "Others made me a slave, but I must squeeze the slave out of myself, drop by drop." Ideology alone could not purge one of the "slave" mentality—the shrinking acquiescence that lined the inside of every woman's psyche. For that, a dig into the interior was necessary.

On that journey to the site of one's own "slave" beginnings—the place where nervelessness was rooted—women struggled to achieve connection with themselves: to gain the strength necessary to shake off the anxieties that prevented them from striking out on their own. In the process, something remarkable was discovered. Standing on your own two feet, you found yourself thinking better, and thinking better, it further developed, reduced the ever-present sense of isolation. Suddenly, you were not alone. You had yourself for company. You had yourself, period. From the Greeks to Chekhov to Elizabeth Cady Stanton, everyone who had ever cared to investigate the nature of human loneliness had seen that only one's own working mind breaks the solitude of the self. A hard truth to look directly into, but the beauty of 70s feminism was that it made thousands prize hard truth over romantic illusion, something very few women were in the habit of doing.

The Queen Is in the Garbage is one of the earliest of those works of literature that, at the end of the 60s, was attempting the archaeological dig into the interior for the sake of emerging with some hard truths. The conceit of the novel is an inner monologue going on in the mind of the protagonist as she tosses about, during fourteen hours of exhausting, premature labor, trying desperately to give birth to the tiny (female) creature within. As a mixture of associative thought and fragmented memories drift repeatedly up into consciousness, we come to realize that she is actually working to puzzle out how it is, exactly, that she has arrived at this moment.

Harriet has grown up the confused and unhappy child of middle-class parents who are themselves unhappy. Marital despair makes the mother vicious. Inevitably, her viciousness is turned on the one who reminds her most of herself. "Everything you touch," she hisses at her daughter, "turns to poison. You've got a rotten mind and rotten blood. That's what you've got. Rotten blood." This is the deadly mantra of the girl's adolescence—and it proves formative. Not only does Harriet experience her mother as punitive and demoralizing; she has come early to fear that her mother's fate might very well be her own. This, she swears fiercely to herself, will never happen. Not because she will do things differently, but because she will do them better. *Her* marriage, she declares, will be marvelous. Thus, Harriet enters into an emotional competition that will, of course, bind her to her mother for life. The rest follows as the night follows the day.

At twenty, Harriet marries a man whose name is the same as her brother's. The marriage is a charade of sibling attachment that ultimately sends them both spinning. One miscarriage and four years later they separate. By now it's the swinging 60s. She travels to Europe and settles in London where, delighting in the rebellious atmosphere, she sleeps around, works at this and that, and, at last, falls in love with an actor whose persistent declarations of love turn neurotically destructive no sooner than the pair have moved in together. Pregnant with the actor's child, and now as unhappy as her mother, Harriet flies home to New York where, one evening at a friend's apartment, she goes unexpectedly into labor. At which point the reader meets her, on an operating table in the city of her birth, pushing for all she's worth to expel the life that she has been choking on.

In the 60s, Harriet was a very recognizable figure: One passed her daily on the streets of every major city in the Western world. She was pretty, bright, somewhat educated, somewhat talented; her ambitions inchoate, her working life without aim or direction, her sense of value ultimately dependent on the positive outcome of a love affair that would "ideally" metamorphose into the marriage that she, in reality, contemplated with split feelings. These feelings went so much against the grain of conventional wisdom that she felt unable to voice them. This young woman was wrapped in a loneliness that had been mapped by many writers, among them George Eliot, Virginia Woolf, Kate Chopin, Jean Rhys. It was the loneliness that grew directly out of an unarticulated inner life. It was a loneliness that, if truth be told, characterized the so-called "emancipated" woman of the 60s every bit as much as it had the protagonists of Woolf, Chopin, Eliot, and Rhys, because not very much had changed in the lives of women during the hundred years or so that these writers and others had been "testifying." The emancipated woman was still being formed by distinctly *un*-emancipated women.

Even more important than the memories of the lover and

the panic his betrayal has brought on, is the stream of associative thought in *The Queen Is in the Garbage* that leads us back again and again to Harriet's mother. It is here, in this knot of primeval attachment, that we find the central relationship of the book, the one, more than any other, that is vitally connected to the protagonist's self-defeating bid for independence. Marked by an intensity of dread and longing, this mother and this daughter seem doomed to repeat one another's lives because both are destined to be ruined by the kind of inner conflict that obviates action. They are locked together in the pain and paradox of their mutual situation. Such mutuality creates intimacy, not love; the kind of intimacy that verges on the ruthless, even the murderous; and murderous impulses, as we all know, are immensely stimulating.

From Oedipus to Freud, our shared notion of the struggle to be in the world has taken its character from the conflict between fathers and sons, a history of violence and urgency that for centuries has described the necessary act of self-assertion. But however fraught the conflict between fathers and sons, essentially it is without ambiguity. The father, compelled as he is to subdue the son, would despise him if he remained behind. The son, anguished as he is over fighting the father, remains undivided in his need to go. He wants the world, and if he must tear flesh and maim spirit to get it, so be it. Life is born out of force and denial at the hands of one's intimates. This is knowledge to be taken in manfully. In fact, the taking in of this knowledge is precisely what has always been called manful.

Henry James—through the women he created—was the first modern writer to observe that in the matter of the world, we are fatally divided against ourselves, at once both attracted and repelled. We advance on the world, we shrink from the world; we want it and fear it at the same time. It is a love affair compromised by the sick excitement of mixed desires.

D.H. Lawrence could taste the dividedness in his mouth. He knew that the obsessiveness between himself and his mother was laced through with fear and desire on a large scale. He could see that it was this relationship, not the one with his father, that was the crucial one in the matter of the world and the divided self. Still, Lawrence was a man, and *Sons and Lovers* was a coming-of-age novel. It was a given that enraged, depressed, unwilling as the protagonist might be, he would nonetheless propel himself *out*.

Throughout this past century, another view of the matter had been clarifying itself across many decades, one that warranted a shift in interest from fathers and sons to mothers and daughters. The necessity, it began to seem, was not so much to kill our fathers as it was to separate from our mothers, and it was the daughters who needed to do the separating. With the daughters, however, the conflict was characterized by crippling ambiguity rather than forward-looking certainty. It's the ambiguity that belongs to the women—and it, too, has had a fictional history as well as an actual one.

Nowhere in literature is there a female equivalent of the protagonist locked in successful struggle with a mother for the sake of the world. Yet a remarkable number of novels exist that detail an *un*successful struggle—May Sinclair's 1919 *Mary Olivier*, Radclyffe Hall's 1924 *The Unlit Lamp*, Virginia Woolf's 1927 *To the Lighthouse*, to name but a fraction—and these are richly informing.

The shock in all of these writings comes from the open declaration of that feeling of erotic murderousness for the one from whom separation seems impossible. We accept rage and ruthlessness as a matter of course in sexual attachment; but when the intimacy is with a parent—especially with a parent of the same sex—the force that these emotions engender seems world-shaking. Yet, no sooner is the insight articulated than the reader calmly thinks, Of course, how could it be otherwise? This, after all, is the intimacy that will bind us all our lives, holding us forever in its thrall, shadowing every other relationship, and determining for a good part, if not all, of our years, our ability to perform the task implicit in all human relations: how to connect yet not merge, how to respond yet not be absorbed, how to detach but not withdraw.

In the 60s it became painfully apparent that these were problems of life—these fearful conflicts over leaving the nest—common to women and men alike. They had been

167

made vivid (emblematic, in fact) in the lives of women only because in women the culture had chosen to exploit the conflicts rather than reduce them—as it had for men; almost deliberately weakening one sex, while strengthening the other, for the sake of what has been perceived, throughout social history, as an immutable need. From Plato on, political philosophers have declared political liberty as fundamental a human necessity as air and food. Yet women, it seemed, did not require it. Women, it was said repeatedly, were, by nature, desirous only of staying home and raising children. And a good thing, too, the philosophers added; otherwise the family would fall apart, and civilization itself would be threatened.

The first time a 70s feminist said, "The personal is political," that famous shock of recognition ran right through the gathering movement for women's rights. It was as though the kaleidoscope of life itself had been shaken, and a new design, surrounded by a new space, could emerge out of old and familiar experience. *The Queen Is in the Garbage* evokes wonderfully what it was like at the end of the 60s for early feminists to feel themselves in the presence of original discovery.

Absorbing viscerally, as well as intellectually, the depth and complexity of that which had most retarded the ability to come into one's own, radical feminists zeroed in on the question of mothers and daughters. Many were struck, as though by lightning, by the perception that it was our

168

mothers (those primary keepers of the culture) who had made us, and that when we had girl children it would be *we* who made *them*. The narrative element in *Queen* that now feels most prescient is the one that has a mother at one end of the protagonist's turmoil and a baby girl at the other. Together, they combine to bring into focus the overweening anxiety of a generation.

When Lila Karp sat down to write her novel, she must have been tasting in her mouth the exhilarating inchoateness that characterized the moment. Leaving Plato's cave, groping in the blinding light for the words and the sentences that would embrace a new emotional syntax—that's what 1969 felt like for thousands; and it is the very thing that *The Queen Is in the Garbage* so beautifully captures. It was a stroke of genius that led Karp to incarnate the time by, on the one hand, having the protagonist, in her semiconscious state, lash out at her mother—I'm not you! I'm not you!—and on the other, bringing her ordeal to an end by letting her deliver a baby who, in a matter of hours, expires: I'm not you, either!

The situation seemed like a slap in the face to middlebrow culture in 1969. It was, however, a wake-up call: one that was destined to be administered many times more, in the years to come, as a storm of novels, memoirs, stories appeared, all somehow crying out, "We are not as you describe us. At this moment, we may not be sure of what we are, but we are certainly aware of what we are not." Enshrined in *The*

Queen Is in the Garbage is the living memory of that historic moment. It is a pleasure to have it back in print.

Vivian Gornick
New York City
February 2007